Beneath the Bridge of Sighs

I0533570

Harriet G. Fry

First Published in 2023 by Blossom Spring Publishing
Beneath the Bridge of Sighs Copyright © 2023 Harriet G. Fry
ISBN 978-1-7395186-3-9
E: admin@blossomspringpublishing.com
W: www.blossomspringpublishing.com

For Emily

Chapter 1

Carol glared at Randy from behind her sunglasses and suppressed the urge to open her mouth.

It's not a canoe! It's a gondola!

Carol knew better than to correct her kid brother out loud. The last thing she wanted was to cause a scene. She would keep her word to Elaine that their time in Venice would remain stress free from start to finish, even with Randy in tow.

"We'll still have a wonderful vacation," Carol had promised her older sister.

Elaine hadn't been so sure.

"What if Randy doesn't like Venice, Carol? Then we'll be stuck with his attitude for two weeks. Remember when he and Joyce broke up? He was such a sour puss!"

Carol remembered, all right. Randy had shown up at her door, duffle bag in hand. He and Joyce were over, he bemoaned. "Could I camp out on your sofa for a few weeks, just until I figure things out? I'll chip in for room and board. I don't want to move back home. Mom might ask too many questions. She was hoping Joyce was 'The One'..."

Carol couldn't have said no even if she'd wanted to. While Elaine liked to refer to Randy as a chronic pain in the butt, Carol saw her bother just as she saw herself: an unlucky in love, but harmless, mutt.

The temporary arrangement worked out in part, the sisters agreed, because Carol worked nights as a registered nurse. Randy, a master carpenter, spent dawn to dusk weekdays on construction sites. They were like two ships passing in the night. While rarely in the same place at the same time, they had made a standing arrangement to meet up on Saturdays for a meal and to catch each other up on their goings on. On Sundays, Carol kept up with her usual household chores, none of which increased due to Randy being there. Both were neat-freaks, Randy pulling his own weight.

From her windows three stories above street level, Carol often noticed that Randy spent most quiet Sunday afternoons walking the perimeter of the little park across the street from her apartment building. His pensive demeanor definitely wasn't that of the Randy she knew and loved. Her brother had always been the life of any party. Didn't he miss Bob's Grill, the SuperPlex Cinema, and Sports Bar Five, his favorite haunts? "Just figuring things out now that Joyce is out of the picture," Randy replied when Carol finally asked why he'd turned into such a homebody. Then, as if an afterthought, Randy volunteered that maybe Joyce was not totally out of the picture after all.

"At least not out of *my* picture, sis. I don't know if I'm totally out of hers, either. But neither of us is picking up the phone."

Carol understood. She knew from experience how first, the heart implodes, bringing with it tears and nail biting and more tears and hair pulling. Then, the head explodes, unleashing all the what-ifs, the sleepless nights re-thinking the turns of events, the twists and tugs of memories competing with the glaring reality: *it's over.* It had taken her so long to feel comfortable dating again after she and her last serious boyfriend, Evan, mutually agreed that *they* were over. Carol was happy for Evan when she learned that he had since met someone new. At the same time, this news found her wondering if there was something wrong with her. Why she couldn't keep a relationship going was a mystery she'd yet to solve. Maybe her brother was feeling the same way. She hoped it wouldn't take Randy long to solve his own mystery.

Three weeks into his sofa-stay, Randy slid into the now-familiar booth in the neighborhood diner where he and Carol met on Saturdays to catch up. Carol was already on her second cup of coffee after ending a non-stop, grueling overnight shift. So many ambulances had arrived at the hospital's ER wing during the night, each carrying a patient with a Friday night injury, accident or illness to treat *stat*. Barroom brawls, auto accidents, overdoses, you name it, Carol saw it. Her calling to work as an ER nurse was true. Carol couldn't see herself in any other setting. Still, it didn't mean she enjoyed the view. She looked forward to having these next two overnights off.

Randy leaned across the table and gave Carol a brotherly peck on the cheek. He was smiling ear to ear.

"I'm starved!" he exclaimed, turning his attention to the menu.

"Is that why you have that grin across your face? What's going on? You look like you *used to* look! Are you and Joyce talking?"

Randy looked up from the menu. "Nope. I know what you're thinking. I'm stoked, though. Really stoked! Let's order first and then I'll spill the beans."

Carol caught a waitress's eye and waved her over. "We'll both have scrambled eggs, wheat toast, home fries, more coffee for me, and decaf for my brother."

Randy held up his hand. "Wait, wait! Yes on the decaf, but I'm not *that* hungry!" His gaze shifted to the waitress's name tag. "Sorry, Donna. My sister always think she knows what I want."

Donna shrugged. "I can come back," she offered.

Carol forced herself not to lift her foot from the floor beneath their table and kick her brother's boot.

"You just told me you were starving," Carol said as calmly as she could. "And I certainly don't think I know what you want. I was just ordering our usual. If you want something different, go ahead. I just want to place my order now." She turned to Donna. "Can you put my order through first? I had a long night. I'm afraid I'll fall asleep right here in the booth if I wait for my brother to make up his mind."

Donna smiled. She offered Randy a quick wink. "I'll be back when you decide, okay?"

Randy shook his head. "Nah, on second thought, I'll just get the same thing except for the toast. I'd like rye. No. Wait. Make it wheat after all. And coffee, decaf.

Wait. No coffee. Make it tomato juice for me."

Carol seethed. *And guys think gals can never make up their minds?*

"My husband does that all the time," Donna volunteered, recognizing Carol's annoyance.

"So do little brothers," Carol replied.

Donna laughed heartily as she turned on her heels and made quick time to the kitchen.

Carol watched her, remembering how she herself scurried all night, from patient to patient in the ER. *We're all on a treadmill*, she thought. Her vacation with Elaine couldn't come soon enough. She leaned back in her seat and frowned at her brother. "So then, if it's not Joyce, what has you so stoked? You haven't shown this side of yourself in weeks."

Randy reached into his jacket pocket and pulled out a little blue booklet. Carol was taken aback. Randy hadn't used his passport since his one and only venture out of the United States, when he'd jumped at the invitation to serve as Best Man for their cousin George's destination wedding. It wasn't until Randy had accepted the honor that he realized that George and Amanda were making their nuptials on a beach in Cancun, Mexico, far enough away from their Trenton, New Jersey hometown to require flying. Randy avoided flying whenever possible. His ears drove him crazy at high altitudes. Even chewing gum, or holding his nose and swallowing, didn't help. Now, here he was, sitting across from her with passport in hand, and smiling no less!

"I'm going to start doing different things, sis. I'm done wondering what Joyce is up to. I want to go with you and Elaine to Italy, and I've got some time off coming in August. That's when you're going, right?"

It was then and there, in the little booth over breakfast with her brother, that Carol broke her half of the promise she and Elaine had made when they first planned their trip: that Venice would be a "just us" getaway, with no tour groups, friends, or relatives in the mix.

Given her brother's circumstances, though, Carol thought Randy's idea was great. As she saw it, he was at the crossroads of marking time and moving forward. He was even willing to board an airplane and put up with the physical discomforts that always came his way at high altitudes. As Carol saw it, Randy was just trying to make a new start, to get back into the excitement of living and exploring new places, maybe even making some new friends along the way. Carol couldn't fault him for that. Her brother was finally ready to shed some old skin. Maybe a trip to Italy was just the thing he needed to get off the emotional merry-go-round, and off of her living room sofa!

***

Now, three months later, here they were, the Duncan trio from Trenton, New Jersey, seated at Caffe La Rosa, a pleasant café they'd come upon while strolling the Via Garibaldi, in this most serene city, as Venice is often claimed to be. Except that Randy was doing everything he could to drive a wedge between Carol and her own serenity. And he didn't even realize it. Carol stifled a sigh as she sipped her cappuccino and listened to her brother rave about gondolas, using all the wrong references. She had to remind herself this was Randy's first time in Venice. She and Elaine had been here before. They had some conversational Italian language skills going in, while their brother was totally clueless. He seemed to be enjoying Venice just the same, though. Carol knew his ignorance of the language was harmless. Besides, he was helping Elaine, carrying her many purchases in many tote bags, through many streets, on foot, of course, this being Venice. His only complaint was having tired feet. Elaine could shop the day away. Carol, on the other hand, was more interested in sightseeing than shopping, and preferred doing so without the lure of shop windows. The sisters had agreed that they'd part company temporarily when their individual interests competed with how much time they had available on a given day's schedule. As for what to do about Randy to keep him from getting antsy, or worse, moping over Joyce, Carol had held out a carrot to Randy in the form of a few extra Euros to spend. All he had to do was help Elaine when she went on her shopping sprees.

Elaine Duncan's home, which she shared with her musician husband Albert Page, and Papa Bear, their loveable senior Springer spaniel, was nothing short of a visual feast of silk and lace and leather and wood and glass, each item displayed with care—and with an invitation to please touch! This trip to Venice would no doubt turn up more treasures for Elaine to take home.

When Carol told Randy that lending some muscle to Elaine's shopping excursions was needed, he had simply shrugged and suggested they rent a car. Poor Randy!

Now that he was here, clogged ears and all, Carol noticed that her brother was at least trying to fit in. He'd quickly come to terms with the fact that cars weren't driven in Venice, rather, water taxis were the way to get around. He seemed to enjoy taking the *vaporetti* up and down the Grand Canal, though he couldn't yet grasp the concept of the *gondola* and hadn't ridden in one yet. Carol decided to treat Randy to a gondola ride before they went home, but only if he stopped calling them canoes. She'd also noticed that her sister's shopping schedule wasn't seriously interrupted by Randy's Italian language faux pas. Elaine was presently engrossed in exploring Venice's fine leather goods shops, in search of a perfect gift for Albert. His birthday was coming up, and Elaine told her she'd planned to replace Albert's cheap plastic billfold with one of genuine leather, hand tooled and stitched, customized with his initials. Of course, Papa Bear had to have a gift from Venice, too, Elaine told her. *Perhaps a new leather leash and harness also hand tooled with his name.* Carol could only imagine how Randy would respond if Elaine were to ask him his opinion on the best-looking designer dog leash. Would he try to talk Elaine out of buying Papa Bear a fancy leash? Randy thought Elaine spoiled the dog too much, though Elaine had confided to Carol more than once that she thought Randy was the spoiled one.

Which reminds me! Carol made a mental note to tell her brother *not* to divulge the source of his extra spending money! Her bribe was strictly between the two of them. She had her own interests in mind as well, when she created the personal porter job for her brother. Carol suspected Randy wouldn't be the least interested in her itinerary, and that suited her just fine. She enjoyed spending time with family, but she liked her solo adventures, too.

There was one place in particular that was at the top of Carol's must-see list: a shop she had not even known existed the last time she visited Venice. After this comfortable respite at Caffe La Rosa, she would bid Elaine and Randy happy shopping, and go on her own to the Libreria Acqua Alta, the high-water bookshop. She just had to check it out after having read an article in a travel magazine about a bookstore in Venice, a literary hideaway that was constructed like no other. She wanted to see for herself that actual books, not mock-ups made to look like books, served as steps stacked tightly together and angled to provide a stairway that led to the shop entrance. How amazing was that! The magazine article also featured a photo of a full-sized bathtub, inside the shop, that served as a symbolic lifeboat for books in the event of *acqua alta,* those high water levels that often flooded Venice's side canals and alleys, not to mention the Piazza San Marco itself, during heavy rains.

While a visit to the Libreria Acqua Alta would be a first for her, Carol had lost count of how many times during her last visit to Venice she'd walked across the Rialto Bridge to the neighborhoods in Dorsoduro Sestiere, marveled at the beautiful dome of the Cathedral of Santa Maria della Salute, and contemplated Jackson Pollack's modern masterpieces at the Guggenheim. And yet, she'd totally missed the *bathtub bookshop* on the other side of the Grand Canal. This visit, Carol was determined to explore the less high-profile landmark sights. This little café, in fact, on the Via Garibaldi, in Venice's Castello Sestiere, or neighborhood, was also a first for her. She had walked the Via Garibaldi before. How could she have bypassed this café? According to the printing on the awning that hung above the entrance to its inside seating area, Caffe La Rosa was established in 1975, twenty years before she was born!

Elaine's words interrupted Carol's quiet reflection. "Let's get going, sis," her sister urged. Carol nodded. She caught their waiter's eye. He approached promptly.

"May I get you anything else, Signorina?"

"Just our check, please, everything was delicious," Carol replied. The waiter smiled broadly and offered a small bow. "Pronto, Signorina, I am happy you and your companions enjoyed your beverages." He walked briskly to the small alcoved entrance beyond the outdoor tables. Carol watched him, feeling warm inside from the melodious lilt of his salutation. Signorina. How lovely the word for *Miss* sounded, coming from the lips of a Venetian gentleman! Carol felt a tingle at the nape of her neck. *Do I dare hope?* She quickly shrugged off her brief fantasy. What was it about being in Venice that made even something as simple as enjoying a cappuccino at an outdoor café, as she was doing now, feel so special? Was it the sunlight reflected on the lagoon, shimmering like gold ribbons formed by the wakes left by passing watercraft, that cast a certain spell? Or, was it something else, something invisible to her eyes, unheard, ephemeral but undeniably real? Everything Carol experienced in beautiful Venice felt perfect, even if Randy's spoken Italian needed work!

Elaine rose from her chair. "I want to freshen up before we go. I'll be right back." She disappeared into Caffe La Rosa's interior and Carol took advantage of being alone with Randy at their outdoor table. "Randy, the extra Euros I'm paying you, Elaine shouldn't know, okay?"

Randy winked. "What Euros, sis?"

Carol shifted in her seat. "Thanks. I just want you to have fun, even when you are working. Elaine takes these shopping excursions very seriously."

Randy laughed. "No kidding! Carrying Elaine's shopping totes is a piece of cake compared to what I do at my day job. I *am* having fun, in my own way. And making some extra money while I do it!" He caught himself. "You didn't hear that!"

"Just make sure Elaine doesn't hear it," Carol replied. She reached under her seat for her purse when she saw the waiter returning to their table with the check.

Randy stood up and fished through his pants pockets, retrieving some of the Euros Carol had given him.

"Everybody's drinks are on me," he announced, loud enough for several patrons seated nearby to hear.

A man at the next table lifted his almost empty wine glass. "Grazie, Signore! Tutti! Everybody! Cheers! Salute!"

Elaine returned from inside the café just in time to witness the debacle her brother initiated. She quickly wove through the tables. A bright smile hid her clenched teeth, as she raised herself on tip toe, applying pressure to Randy's shoulder with her hand. He leaned to one side to give her his ear.

"Sit down and be quiet. *Now*," Elaine hissed before lowering herself to her heels and demurely settling back in her chair. She turned in her seat to face the cluster of gleeful patrons who were waiting with raised glasses for Randy to make good on his generous gesture.

"Excuse our brother, everyone. He is just so excited to be here." She lowered her eyes as she placed her hand over her heart. "He means well. Please accept our apologies."

The patrons lowered their glasses. One man spoke up, shaking his head in disappointment. "Americani, tutti pazzi!" *All crazy Americans!* Carol watched all of this as if in an audience, leaving it to Elaine to clean up Randy's verbal mess.

Their waiter stood by, poker faced while Randy dug further into his pockets for more Euros.

"I want to pay the check but it looks like I'm a little short," Randy muttered. He turned to the waiter. "Sig Noro, do you take credit cards?" Before the waiter could answer, Carol handed him some of her Euros, and Elaine followed suit. They also insisted the waiter keep the change, which amounted to a very generous tip. It was the least they could do after all the commotion Randy caused. The entire transaction seemed to go right over Randy's head.

"Look at my sisters, treating me like I'm a kept man!" Randy joked to the waiter.

The waiter thanked them, bowed quickly, turned on his heels, and fled. Talk about the end of a romance, if only an imagined one. Carol flinched, embarrassed for the poor man having to put up with their brother's off-center sense of humor.

Randy turned to his sisters. "Did I say something wrong to that guy? I was just, you know, trying to make him smile."

Elaine glared at her brother. "You scared that poor soul out of his wits, Randy." He'll probably go home tonight and tell his family about us. Not that it matters, but we'd better get out of here."

"I second that!" Carol chimed. She pulled herself up from her chair. Randy's antics had put an end to her thoughts of coming back to Caffe La Rosa. As welcomed as she first felt being here, Carol suspected that, at least on some level, she and Randy and Elaine were collectively black-listed for being *crazy Americans*. Carol still had her sights set on checking out the Libreria Acqua Alta before the day was over, and she wasn't going to let Randy's behavior get in the way of that.

The trio left the café and made their way down the Via Garibaldi until its wide pavement spilled onto Riva degli Schiavoni waterfront expanse that stretched parallel to the Grand Canal along the edge of Castello Sestiere. Before going separate ways, Randy, Elaine and Carol coordinated their next meeting point, agreeing to meet up at two o'clock, at Carol's destination, the Libreria Acqua Alta. Randy and Elaine took a path along a narrow quay, or fondamenta, that led to another shopping venue. Carol headed out alone, deeper into the twists and turns of

Venice's interior alleys.

Someone else was alone, too, following the trio unnoticed, as he'd done the day before.

Chapter 2

The woman was a mirror image of Leonora, and Sergio Bari hadn't been able to take his eyes off of her since the first time he saw her. But she could not be Leonora. There had been a time long ago, Sergio remembered as if it were yesterday, when he and Leonora Santella were young and in love. But those days were long gone.

The dark hairs on the back of his neck always stood up, as they did now, whenever he recalled those midnights in the Campo Bandiera e Moro. There, he and Leonora huddled between two thick bushes in the Campo's garden, careful not to cast shadows as they embraced.

Where she was now, Sergio could only guess. A decade had passed since Leonora left Venice for a new life, to train as a flight attendant with an international airline based on the other side of the world. Sergio still remembered Leonora's explanation practically word for word, when she broke the news to him that she was leaving Venice, leaving him. She had told him she had to go, that she was nineteen years old with only a high-school education. How she hated her job sitting all day in a cubicle answering phones and listening to customer complaints. She'd started crying then, Sergio remembered. His heart still ached when he thought of how she took his hands, held them to her cheeks, and let him dry her tears with his fingertips. He would have married her then and there if he could have, but it would never be. Leonora Santella was already married, to a dream. A dream that didn't include him. Her last lament had said it all, as they huddled in the bushes on what was to be their last night together. *Why was I born here, in a city that is sinking into the lagoon millimeter by millimeter? Why couldn't I have been born in New York, or in Paris, or London? Why Venice? I'm afraid I'll never get out if I don't do it now, and not in New York, or Paris.*

To this day, Sergio remembered how he nodded dumbly as her monologue stabbed him, one memory at a time. What was wrong with this place? It was the most beautiful city one could imagine, people flocked from all over the world to see Venice. She was, to Sergio, the jewel of the Adriatic. He never had a desire to live anywhere else. That night, in the Campo, he hadn't defended Venice and, in not doing so, had not defended himself against Leonora's laments. *I understand*, he finally told her, for lack of knowing what else to say. He'd understood nothing of what pulled Leonora out of his arms that night. He could hardly bear to wipe her tears from his fingertips after she kissed him one last time then disappeared into the night as she ran from the Campo toward a place that was anywhere but here.

Leonora's departure had left him stunned. Was he too old fashioned or maybe too narrow-minded never to have considered that Leonora might have wanted more out of life? He nonetheless held out hope that Leonora Santella would change her mind, and so he showed up at the Campo each night for two weeks. When Leonora failed to appear, he took a bold step and sought out her mother. Even this, Sergio recalled as though it were yesterday.

Signora Santella, like Sergio, had hoped her daughter would remain at home until she married, though whomever she married, Sergio was sure, would have to pass the Signora's inspection. Italian mothers were very careful about that sort of thing, especially if they were raising their daughters alone, as the Signora was doing. She had been widowed since Leonora was a young child.

Signora Santella had answered Sergio's knock on her

door, at first eyeing him cooly. She eventually invited him in. Their common thread was concern for Leonora. Signora Santella promised Sergio that the next time Leonora contacted her, she would tell him, but had made it clear that it would be up to Leonora to contact him herself. Sergio saw his own predicament reflected through the mirror of the Signora's spoken sentiments.

"My daughter, she has big ideas, Sergio. She is an adult. I could not force her to stay. I can only pray she will be safe when she flies. Never will I need to fly far away. Everything I need is here. I stay where I am."

Sergio had left Leonora's family home that evening convinced that Signora Santella would not contact him if Leonora ever came home. He didn't know why he felt that way, but he trusted his gut.

Sergio never visited Leonora's family home again. He never received a phone call. With the passage of time, Sergio let go of hope that he and Leonora would find each other again.

In the years after he completed university, he pivoted to the lifestyle of a swinging single, and he learned to enjoy it for all it was worth. Sergio could be seen every weekend, escorting an attractive date—rarely the same lady twice—to Venice's hottest night spots for dancing and drinks, or attending concerts and films, and, in the warm months, swimming on the Lido. Eventually, his parents retired, leaving Sergio to manage the family business, the Caffe La Rosa. With his Business Management degree, coupled with real world experience having worked in the café since his teens, learning the ropes from prep cooking to cleanup and everything in between, Sergio had now been running Caffe La Rosa for three years on his own, and as successfully as his parents had for so many years before passing the baton to their only child.

Sergio's management duties actually proved to be less time consuming than his parents had experienced, given today's modern technology. Caffe La Rosa still held its charm, and attracted many patrons, local regulars and tourists alike, for both private dining indoors, and outdoor refreshment and people-watching. The difference these days was in the paperwork. There was virtually none. Recordkeeping tasks, from payroll to reservations, and everything in between, were stored "in the Cloud" and, while Sergio was always the first to show up to open for the day and the last to leave at night, he had dedicated, computer savvy staff to keep pace with La Rosa's daily business operations. Still, nothing took the place of the personal touch of extending a smile and a greeting to the many visitors to his café. That's why Sergio relished his late mornings there. He most enjoyed sitting at his small, private table just outside the restaurant's entrance, facing the outdoor café, sipping espresso and watching the people go by. Just as he was doing the day before yesterday, when the beautiful, tall, dark-haired woman appeared with her two companions. The threesome had taken an outdoor table at his café and the tall woman, her back to him, was quietly people-watching and sipping cappuccino on the Via Garibaldi.

The tall woman's companions faced him: a short lady, cute, plump, bespeckled. She shared the same dark brown hair as the tall woman, but wore hers shorter, in a modern, asymmetrical cut. A young man completed the trio. He was as tall as the beautiful long-haired woman, with biceps that hinted he did a lot of physical labor. He wore his lighter brown hair buzz cut, close to his scalp, and his turned-up nose matched that of the cute plump lady. Sergio considered they might be related. Brother and sisters, maybe. Or perhaps cousins. What he was absolutely sure of was that they were tourists. *American* tourists.

At the table, the young man had stacked many tote bags, each filled to bursting, beneath his and the plump lady's chairs. Sergio chuckled at the sight. The tourists' love of shopping seemed to be what kept Venice's economy going. Sergio was glad Venice had so many visitors, spending their Euros and swiping their credit cards. At the same time, he hoped that visitors to his city would take time to appreciate more of what the city had to offer than just its tangibles. She had so much history! Sergio always thought of Venice as female, like a ship, and why not? Was she not a city on the water? *In* the water? To Sergio, Venice had multiple personalities: demure and haughty, decadent and holy. She had something for everyone. He thought that, if non-Venetians could *become* Venetians, if only temporarily, by going off the beaten path, assimilating with the locals, rather than simply spending their Euros, they might return home with richer memories of this beautiful city, his home. As Sergio observed the goings on at the table with the two ladies and the young man, he wondered if they would make the time to explore the Venice that mattered most: its heart and soul.

The tall woman was obviously enjoying the view on the Via Garibaldi, and didn't appear interested in her companions' preoccupation with the stacks of tote bags beneath their table. Sergio smiled slightly. *Very nice people*, Sergio thought, even if that cute little plump lady in the eyeglasses and the lanky young man may be addicted to shopping. The tall woman with them had no tote bags under her chair, Sergio noticed. Just then, the tall woman turned in her seat. Sergio's breath caught in his throat.

Time slammed to a stop. Even the melodious ring coming from his mobile phone inside didn't distract Sergio from the sight of the woman, who was now standing, facing him, smoothing her skirt. Her companions were gathering their belongings, preparing to leave.

Sergio stared straight ahead; his eyes locked on the beauty before him. *Leonora!* He wanted to call out her name, but held his tongue. This woman was not Leonora Santella. But she could have been. His phone still ringing, Sergio ignored it. The beautiful stranger standing before him, in one split second, had erased his long held conviction that there was no such phenomena as every person on Earth having a double, a "twin" lookalike, somewhere in this world.

Yet, here she was, Leonora Santella's "twin", identical from her flowing dark brown hair that matched the color of her eyes, to her Aquiline nose, her pouting lips, and a complexion that can only be compared to porcelain, just like Leonora's. The beautiful stranger's legs stretched seemingly forever from the hem of her white linen summer skirt, like those of the young man through his well-worn jeans. But that was where their similarities ended. The man had the impish features and lighter brown hair and eyes of the short plump woman with the many totes. They all had something in common with one or the other, so they must be related, Sergio decided. That made sense. A Leonora Santella twin, on the other hand, made no sense. His Leonora had been an only child. There was no twin, unless one believed the old adage. Sergio had no choice but to believe it now. There she was. And he couldn't take his eyes off of her.

Sergio was not a tall man himself, but such a minor difference was of no concern to him. His Leonora was taller than he was. And it never mattered to either of them when they were young and in love. Would her twin find this difference uncomfortable? Sergio scolded himself. *This lady doesn't even know you! And you don't know her!*

He took a few deep breaths. He decided he should at least thank her for coming to his café. He'd thank the short plump woman and the tall young man, too, for their patronage at his café.

His phone had stopped ringing and only now, as he rose from his chair, did he remember that his best friend Paolo Trezzi, had told him to expect a call from him this morning. Sergio saw that the call had come from Paolo.

When he looked up from his phone, Leonora's lookalike was gone.

Chapter 3

Elaine stepped onto the narrow footbridge spanning a quiet, side canal. She looked over her shoulder to be sure Randy was still with her. They stopped midpoint on the footbridge to take in the tranquil scene. A lone gondola swayed from its mooring just below. The gondolier sat on the craft's red velvet bench, a Bluetooth in his ear, his eyes closed, fingers tapping against the vessel's smooth lacquered hull.

"I guess he's on his lunch break," Randy said.

The gondolier opened his eyes, smiled, and closed them again.

"Randy, I could swear we were being followed when we left the Via Garibaldi," Elaine whispered, careful not to disturb the napping gondolier.

"By that guy in the canoe?" Randy asked loudly enough that the dozing gondolier opened his eyes again. This time, though, he didn't smile at the twosome.

"Stop it, Randy!" Elaine hissed under her breath. "You're embarrassing me!"

Randy turned his back to the canal and whispered into his sister's ear. "Okay, okay. Is this better?"

Elaine shooed him away. "Just try to keep your voice down, please." Elaine motioned in the direction they had traveled to get to the footbridge. "Did you notice anybody back there?"

Randy shook his head. "Nope, all I notice is my arms. They're falling out of their sockets." He looked down at the pile of tote bags at his feet. Even if it meant waking up that guy in the canoe, stopping here on the footbridge allowed for a chance to unload his burden and rest his limbs. What was it about women and shopping? Even Joyce used to… Randy shuddered. *For crying out loud, man, forget Joyce*, he silently admonished himself, yet knowing full well he couldn't do such a thing. Randy nonetheless forced himself to try, at least while he was with Elaine. His sister looked him up and down, exasperation written all over her face, her ample, freckled arms folded over her chest. She pursed her lips like a school teacher waiting for an unruly student to settle down. Randy couldn't help but smile. Even when she tried to look serious, his older sister couldn't fool him, and she knew it, too.

"So, you ordered Albert's custom billfold and it will be ready tomorrow, right?" Randy asked, changing the subject. Elaine's serious expression melted at once.

"Yes! I can't wait to give it to him. You know, I miss him a lot, Randy. The only thing that takes my mind off of being away from him is all of this!" She waved her chubby fingers over one of her totes. "The lace table runners are in this one," she said, then, pointing to a larger tote. "I have the carnival masks, the Murano glass figurines and the carved marionette in this one."

"What are you going to do with a puppet?" Randy asked.

Elaine shrugged. "I don't know yet. But it was gorgeous, handmade, and the price was right. I had to have it. Now, don't change subjects on me, little brother, did you or didn't you notice if we were being followed back there?

"We weren't being followed, not that I could tell," Randy replied. "But seriously, sis, can we maybe take a half day off from shopping today, maybe call it quits after lunch? My arms are really sore, I'm not kidding. I need to soak in a hot bath." They'd been on their feet since nine o'clock this morning and only stopped once to sit down for a beverage at Caffe La Rosa. Elaine had to admit that Randy had been a good sport, trekking the alleys and footbridges with her from one shop or stall to another.

"You win," she said, her tone feigning disappointment. "But just know that I overheard you tell Carol that you lift lumber all day at your work sites, that these totes weigh nothing in comparison."

Randy started to protest but held his tongue. His sister had him.

"Okay, Elaine, go ahead. One more shop. I'll stay here on the foot bridge and..." Suddenly Randy stopped speaking. He cocked his head. "Wait a sec."

"Wait for what?" Elaine asked. "You just said I could..."

Randy held up his hand. "Shhh. Listen. Did you hear that? Sounds like a cry..."

He turned, stepped over the totes, and started back across the foot bridge.

Elaine waited for Randy to return. Whatever her brother had just heard, she had not. He was off the bridge now, walking partway down the narrow alley from which they came before returning to his sister.

"Go ahead to your last shop, I'll stay here. If you buy anything too heavy, wave to me. I'll come help you."

Elaine didn't move. "What was it you thought you

heard?"

"It sounded like Carol," Randy said. "But it couldn't have been. She's too far from here."

The dozing gondolier snorted loudly.

"Ooops," Randy whispered, motioning to the gondola still moored beneath the foot bridge. "I forgot about him. Maybe that's who I heard."

Together they stood in silence waiting, but for what, or for whom, they didn't know. Suddenly, a figure emerged from yet another alley that led to the footbridge.

Elaine grabbed Randy's arm, pulling him up off his haunches. "Randy, look! I think it's Carol!"

Sure enough, Carol was heading their way, and the look on her face gave both Elaine and Randy a bone-chilling scare. The last shop on Elaine's agenda was forgotten as she and Randy rushed back across the footbridge to their sister.

"It... it was cl-closed..." Carol gasped, falling into Elaine's open arms. She breathed deeply to settle herself as best she could before trying to say more.

To Randy and Elaine, the short wait felt like an eternity. "What happened back there?" Randy implored. "Was somebody following you?"

Carol finally spoke. "Libreria Acqua Alta had a sign on its door. *Chiudo*. Closed. But somebody was watching me from close by. I didn't see anybody. I can't explain it. But I *felt* it. I got scared, I started running, calling out." Carol took another deep breath. Someone was watching me. I am absolutely sure of it. I'm just so relieved I found you…"

Elaine rummaged through her purse. She retrieved a handkerchief and wiped the beads of sweat that had formed on Carol's face.

"It's all right, sis, we'd have found *you* one way or the other," Elaine assured.

Randy spoke up, "Elaine thought somebody was following her, too."

Instinctively, Carol reached out to Elaine and drew her close as if to shield them both from some mysterious boogieman.

"Where? Did you see them?"

Before Elaine could open her mouth, Randy was spilling the story. "It was just before we got here. Elaine thought she heard something, and she thought somebody was following her, and then I heard something. But I heard you. I don't know what or who was following

Elaine. Let's just go back to the hotel. This is a girl thing. I think you both are letting Venice's twists and turns get the best of you!"

Elaine ignored Randy's remark. She gently pulled herself from Carol's grasp. She offered her sister her side of the story.

"From just before we got here to the foot bridge, we... I mean I, had gone into a few shops already, and Randy was right behind me, carrying my stuff. He waited outside each shop while I went in. But he said he didn't see or hear anything."

Randy nodded. "Affirmative. Like I said, this is a girl thing. I have nothing to add, except can we go back to the hotel now?"

"Our little brother thinks we are just a couple of hysterical old crows," Elaine said as she and Carol smoothed their hair and checked their clothes. "Do I have footbridge dust on me?" she asked Carol.

"No, you're good," Carol replied. "Do I?"

"You're good," Elaine said. "Let's go, guys." She reached for her totes.

Randy intervened, beating Elaine to the totes. He rolled his eyes. "Footbridge dust? *I* was the one sitting on the footbridge. Ask me about *my* dust!"

Elaine winked at Carol. "Too bad our strong lumber-carrying brother's arms hurt so much. He could have fought off whoever was following us. But maybe that's why he wants us to think we are imagining things. It gives *him* an excuse *not* to defend us, but without having to admit that he's not as strong as he thinks he is."

Randy scowled. "You both just get too weird on me sometimes, like you believe in ghosts."

Carol turned to her brother. "Actually, Venice has ghosts. There is even a walking tour called Haunted Venice. It starts from the Piazza San Marco and follows all of Casanova's escapades through the city."

Randy grunted. "So? What's that supposed to mean?"

"It means that I believe the *ghost* of Giacomo Casanova is constantly roaming around Venice. Maybe Elaine and I are feeling Casanova's spiritual vibes." Elaine turned to Carol. "From what I've read about Casanova, he did leave his mark on this city. He certainly loved the ladies. Maybe you're onto something, sis."

Randy groaned. "I mean it, you two! Let's go back to the hotel. I'm done playing pack mule for the day. And I'm not going ghost busting, either!" He walked ahead of them, shaking his head, thinking how much he missed his car. And Joyce. He knew he wouldn't find either in Venice. He wondered what Joyce was doing now. Had she started seeing other guys? Or was she still feeling down in the dumps some days, as he was? How could he know? And why *should* he know? He wasn't texting Joyce, and she hadn't sent him any texts, either. They'd gone their separate ways on all fronts ever since the night before he had shown up at Carol's door.

A new sound, coming from a narrow alley, interrupted Randy's thoughts as he and his sisters continued on their way through the streets and alleys that would eventually lead them to a fondamenta that merged with the Riva degli Schiavoni and the Grand Canal. There was little foot traffic now. People were settling in for their mid-day meal and respite. More people would be walking around would pick up again after seven o'clock in the evening as the shops reopened and locals and tourists promenaded on the vast expanse of Piazza San Marco. Venice kept late hours.

What could this new sound be, then, if there was nobody around? Could his sisters be right? Could it be that Venice really was haunted? And who was this dude,

Casanova, who was supposed to be so hot? There it was again! The sound reminded him of windchimes, but there were no windchimes swaying from balconies or doorways.

"Randy, come on, keep up with us before you lose us," Elaine called over her shoulder.

"I'm with you, don't worry," Randy said, picking up his pace. "I just thought I heard something... or someone..."

"Well, Randy, maybe Casanova is trying to talk to you, too," Elaine called back, not slowing her pace.

"If he is, I can use some pointers on how to be a ladies' man," Randy answered.

Carol and Elaine exchanged knowing glances. *That's what our kid bro needs, an encounter with Giacomo Casanova!*

"Elaine and I are all in for taking that Haunted Venice walking tour, how about you?" Carol asked her brother.

Randy thought, *Why not?* If Joyce didn't want him anymore, maybe he'd meet somebody special right here in Venice. But he wouldn't meet anyone just sitting in his hotel room with his feet up, which was what he'd planned to do tonight.

"Yeah, I'll go," Randy replied.

"Great!" Carol squealed. "Maybe you'll catch the Casanova spell!"

Randy winced. "I don't want to catch anything from him. Who is he, anyway?"

Before Carol could answer, Elaine tugged at Randy's arm. "We're here," she announced, pointing to the hotel as she picked up her pace. "Come on, slowpoke!"

Randy flinched. "Easy! I told you my arms feel like bricks."

Elaine slowed down and relieved Randy of her totes. "Who was the one who wanted to get back here so early in the day? I'll take it from here."

Randy shook his arms and rotated his wrists. "I need a hot soak in the tub. What time do you want me to meet you for that haunted walk thing?"

"You really want to go, then?" Elaine asked him.

"Do you think your tired feet will be able to keep up with Giacomo Casanova?" Carol joked.

"Yep and yep," Randy said. "So, when do we do this?"

They agreed to meet up at seven in the lobby. As he rode the elevator up to his floor, Randy remembered the sound he'd heard earlier. He decided it was nothing. *I've got to stop channeling those two, he thought. I'm getting out on my own after tonight. Tomorrow morning, I submit my resignation!*

***

Carol called room service. When their carafe of red wine arrived, along with a sumptuous platter of cheese and fruit, the Duncan sisters settled in for an afternoon chat sans Randy. This was the first time since their brother had made a scene at Caffe La Rosa that they were able to talk alone.

"I think Randy is considering trying his luck with the ladies again," Carol ventured.

"Me, too," Elaine said. "I just hope he isn't setting his hopes too high. You know, being on the rebound."

Carol nodded. "I remember when you were on the rebound. It wasn't until you stopped giving your heart away on every first date that you…"

"And what about you and Evan?" Elaine interrupted as she leaned over the plate of cheese and fruit, perusing the selections. She raised an eyebrow before plucking a grape from the plate. Neither of us has the right to counsel our brother on starting over. I retired my old heart throb Frank Delaney. Remember him?

Carol smiled. "I sure do. I thought you and Frank made a great couple."

Elaine sighed, remembering. "We did. But we didn't fit in the ways that counted most." She leaned forward as though preparing to impart some deep dark secret.

"And what were those ways?" Carol asked, though she didn't have to. Carol knew the reasons her sister and Frank didn't end up married. They'd talked about it so many times, Carol could recite Elaine's words as if they were her own. But they liked to play this little game when they discussed their exes. Besides, it looked good with the wine and cheese, two ladies, heads together in gossip, holding long-stemmed glasses of vino rosso, looking so…so…*so, what?* The wine was getting to both of them. They burst out laughing in unison.

"When will Carol Duncan retire Evan Grayson?" Elaine whispered through a wide grin.

Carol shrugged. "Did I retire him, or fire him? I don't remember!"

Elaine giggled. "Evan either got a pink slip, or you

gave him the slip."

"I just don't think marriage is in the cards for me," Carol said. "Not that I don't hope it is. But if it doesn't happen, that's okay, too." She raised her glass to her sister. "To you and Albert, and to Randy and whomever, someday!"

Elaine tipped her glass. "And to you, sis. No matter what, just enjoy every minute. I'm glad we did this."

"So am I." Carol helped Elaine clean their fruit and cheese plate. She was glad for this mid-day respite, just the two of them and no Randy, like it was originally planned. But it had been her idea to include him, and Carol was glad Elaine didn't seem to mind. They'd all meet up again for the Haunted Venice tour later this evening, and they'd have a great time. In fact, Carol felt up for experiencing just about any surprises Venice had to offer just to shake off that creepy feeling she'd had outside the Libreria Acqua Alta. Even now, in the safety and comfort of their hotel, Carol sensed someone watching her every move.

Chapter 4

Sergio pressed the snooze button on his alarm clock, turned himself away from the window, and pulled the covers over his head. If there was ever a morning he didn't want to have to get out of bed, this was it. The argument with his better angel against following the three American tourists had won out. Sergio promised himself that it wouldn't happen again. So what if the lovely tall woman looked exactly like his long gone Leonora Santella? Even if he had managed to strike up a conversation with the trio, would he have had the opportunity to separate them so that he could speak with the lady alone? He'd failed to catch her eye at his café, and then lost his nerve when he spotted her a half hour later outside the shuttered Libreria Acqua Alta. Instead, he had stood in the recessed doorway of another shop until she suddenly broke into a trot, then a full-on sprint, disappearing again until last evening when he saw her again.

He had to thank his best friend, Paolo Trezzi, known only to most tourists as Giacomo Casanova, for providing an unexpected third opportunity. Such good luck that the same three Americans he'd paid such attention to yesterday had also decided to meet on the Piazza San Marco for Paolo Trezzi's popular group walking tour the very evening he had promised Paolo he'd also show up for the performance. Could the timing have been any better? Was it fate?

Sergio had participated in the walking tour in the past. It was so entertaining even locals like himself, who already knew all about Casanova, showed up to take the brisk hour-long walk within the safety of a group. Paolo had played his part brilliantly, as usual, capturing the essence of the true Giacomo Casanova of centuries past. At the conclusion of the walk through the famous haunts of Venice's most famous seducer, Sergio had come away with the assumption that his Leonora lookalike had to be unmarried. In his conventional way of thinking, Sergio considered the traditional band of gold proof positive that a woman was married. No ring, no vow taken. An old-fashioned way of thinking, he knew, but his way nonetheless. The lady's delicate fingers, he'd noticed last evening, were unadorned. He was hopeful that this meant he might strike up an acquaintance with her, unencumbered. But wasn't he encumbering himself?

How could he, a popular, well-liked business owner and man about town, suddenly be so shy and tongue tied?

Like all cities, Venice was not without its intrigue after dark. Sergio had a voice message from Paolo to meet at Bibi's Bar after the walking tour. The message certainly intrigued Sergio: Paolo "had news" to relay. Sergio could only guess what the news could be. But he didn't try. His best friend was always in the thick of things. Whatever news Paolo had under his cap, Sergio knew it wouldn't be mere gossip. It would be something that involved Paolo directly. And the news would be happy. Sergio couldn't remember a time when his friend looked at life through any other lens. Paolo's onstage and offstage personalities were often indistinguishable, and last night had been no exception. Paolo had brought Giacomo Casanova to life with his usual charm and wit, translating the famous 18th-century Italian lover's every gesture and nuance, portraying him as not just a heartthrob, but as an astute, thoughtful and intelligent young man of his time, yet still holding that special *come to me* gleam in his eyes.

As he dressed for the day, Sergio thought about last evening's tour, from the period costume Paolo wore—

cape, leotard, lace-edged shirt sleeves, ruffled collar, and a cap that sat atop shoulder length hair that Paolo grew specifically for his role—to the audience responses to Paolo's narratives, gestures, and jokes. Paolo had once told Sergio that, each time he put on his costume, he reminded himself that Casanova had both a light and a serious side, and that the audience should be introduced to both on his Haunted Venice walking tour. Last night had been no exception, but, clearly, the audience gravitated more toward Casanova's fabled "bad boy" traits. With his experience as an actor, Paolo could size up an audience in minutes, and his observations had told him to go light on his character's serious side, and heavy on the juicy stuff, such as Casanova's clandestine meetings with the maidens who lived as nuns within the walls of Venice's convents!

Paolo's finely tuned Casanova monologue, embellishing the narrative with his own interpretation of his alter-ego's flirtatious glances, brought squeals of delight from the ladies in the audience on the receiving end, save for one short, chubby lady who raised both of her hands to her lips, suppressing a gasp. The poor woman was evidently shocked to learn that the cloistered religious were among Casanova's most prolific romantic conquests! Another woman —she looked like someone Paolo couldn't immediately place but had a feeling he'd seen before—had cupped her own hands to whisper into the ear of her shocked companion. The chubby lady's shocked expression softened, then morphed into one of sheer glee, with both ladies bursting into hearty laughter that blended with that of the others in the group. Paolo's audience last night was in a partying mood, to say the least, and Casanova didn't let them down!

Sergio was able to witness all of this from his vantage point in the audience of women, one of whom was Leonora's lookalike. It was she who had whispered into the ear of the plump woman. The only other man in the audience was their male companion, who seemed to be studying Paolo's physical movements as he maneuvered himself between and around the group to get the best views. Paolo swung his oil lantern and cast shadows below the marble arches of the Doge Palace, then switching direction to skip quickly to another place, then another, before ending up at their starting point beneath the columns of Saint Mark's symbolic lions. The tour concluded with Paolo's Casanova kissing the hands of the ladies in his audience and bowing formally to the two men in the group, before taking his leave to a round of applause, and pocketing some very generous tips. It had been *una buona notte*!

The group splintered off into different directions. Sergio watched the tall lady and her companions walk toward a trattoria. Mandolin melodies escaped through an opened door. The threesome entered the trattoria and, once again, Sergio had missed his chance to talk to the woman who had stopped his heart mid-beat just twelve hours earlier. He was suddenly exhausted, and it was all he could do to force himself to make good on his agreement with Paolo to meet for a drink at the conclusion of the Haunted Venice walking tour, and to hear Paolo's news.

Preparing his morning espresso now, Sergio smiled, recalling how he had walked to Paolo's neighborhood with the same quick pace, but without the stealth he'd applied to his movements when he'd followed the beautiful Leonora lookalike to the Libreria Acqua Alta. Paolo had beat Sergio to Bibi's and had already tagged two bar stools when Sergio showed up. Paolo had chided Sergio for looking like a sleuth with his shirt collar pulled up almost to his ears.

Sipping his espresso at his kitchen table, Sergio replayed the sensation of a sudden chill that had gone through his body on the walk to Bibi's. He'd let Paolo kid him about looking like Sherlock Holmes. He'd laughed off Paolo's remark and turned his attention to the drinks Paolo had ordered for them. It had felt good to be at Bibi's with his best friend. The tourists hadn't yet discovered this little capsule-sized gem, which was good for Paolo and his family given they lived above the bar. Sergio also knew that, as much as his friend appreciated the tourist trade for his livelihood, Paolo preferred spending his time with his wife and children. Last night, Paolo hadn't even changed out of his Casanova attire. He'd ordered two shots of anisette, offered a toast of *buona fortuna*, then hit Sergio with the news, taking the roundabout way to do so.

"If the rent weren't so reasonable here, I'd move Anna and the twins to Lido for some breathing room."

Sergio had nodded. Paolo wasn't going to move to Lido Beach, he knew. He loved living in the heart of Venice.

"I was afraid, though, that Enzo, our landlord, would

raise the rent once he knew another person would be living here." A half hour and several refills of anisette later, they were deep into toasting Anna Trezzi's pregnancy. When all was said and done, Paolo had filled Sergio in on the details of the landlord's generous offer to paint all of the rooms in Paolo and Anna's apartment in preparation for their third child. They'd raised another toast, too: to Sergio being Godfather to the baby. Such an honor!

Sergio locked the door of his apartment behind him and walked to his vaporetto stop. Paolo, filled with excitement at sharing his happy news of a new baby on the way, had almost sidetracked him from voicing his own reason for agreeing to meet up with his friend last night. It was only when Paolo had kidded that Anna might lock him out of their bedroom if he didn't get upstairs soon to eat his dinner and spend time with the twins before their bedtime, did Sergio remember to tell his friend about the beautiful stranger. Boarding the vaporetto, he mentally recited the last thing they talked about before wrapping up the evening.

"Remember Leonora Santella, my old girlfriend?"

Paolo nodded. "You told me she left you to go

to work overseas."

"That's right."

"I never met her."

"Right, she was gone by the time you moved to Venice. It doesn't seem like that long ago, but it was."

"You told me a lot about her. You still think of her, yes?"

Sergio had found himself in a mental time machine then. Details about Leonora flooded up from the depths of time, how she often liked to dress "like a movie star", piling her hair high atop her head and wearing high heels. She liked to *dress tall*, she had told him. In heels and high hair styles, she had succeeded in appearing taller than he was, Sergio remembered. It had not bothered him at all, yet, with hindsight, he'd wondered if she had done such a thing because she liked the look, or because she wanted to appear superior in some way. In any case, what did it matter?

Paolo had remembered this, too, from Sergio's long ago stories of the young woman who had taken a direction that would take her so far away, perhaps for good.

Paolo had also reminded him that he had been born in

Genoa and that, by the time he arrived in Venice, Sergio was already living the life as one of the city's most eligible bachelors, while he, Paolo Trezzi, had willingly clipped his bachelor's wings to wed Anna Dorio from Milan. They had no roots in Venice, no history, and had moved there for the romance of the place, why else? No, Leonora Santella was only a memory by proxy. Neither Paolo nor Anna had ever met her. Only Sergio's stories had brought Leonora Santella to life, and that was a long time ago.

Sergio had sent Paolo a text when he arrived home, inviting him to breakfast this morning at his café. They could sober up after all their celebratory toasts at *Bibi's*, Sergio added good naturedly. Paolo hadn't sent a return text last night, but as Sergio disembarked the vaporetto at the Arsenale stop, his phone rang with the familiar text notification tone. It was Paolo: *I bet you three cups of espresso and a plate of biscotti that I will beat you to Via G today!*

Sergio picked up his pace. Turning onto Via Garibaldi, he could see Paolo waiting outside Caffe La Rosa. As soon as he took care of Paolo's breakfast, he'd place a bet of his own: that his best friend would agree that, last evening on the Piazza San Marco, Sergio had seen Leonora Santella, even if nobody else did.

Chapter 5

Sergio frowned. "But you play a ladies man, Paolo. You play Giacomo Casanova. Are you living through him, playing the field, as you call it, without being unfaithful to your wife?"

Paolo slapped his free hand on the table top and grinned as he brought his cup of espresso to his lips. "Now that's an analogy if I ever heard one, my friend!" he laughed, then in a single gulp downed the rich coffee. "Ah, perfecto! Best espresso outside of my Anna's kitchen! But to your question, no! *My* Casanova only flirts, he brings nobody upstairs, not even in his fantasies. But you are still on the dance floor, yes?"

Sergio's frown melted. He was, but he didn't want to admit it. He shrugged off Paolo's question. "It doesn't matter. But I was at home last Saturday night."

"So was I," said Paolo. "I danced with my Anna when the twins fell asleep. And after we danced, we loved each other as only spouses could understand. You, on the other hand, collect women for all the wrong reasons. You do not commit, my friend. Sometimes I think, 'Sergio will end up alone in his old age'. That bothers me."

Paolo's words stung. Sergio spoke up. "Wait a minute, it's true that I—"

"Hear me out," Paolo interrupted. You wined and dined many women, you enjoyed having fun with them, but you never loved any one of them. Your first love you could not have, and so, all this time, you have never given yourself a second chance to find true love. Always in the back of your mind, it was Leonora you waited for. You are still waiting for her, even though you are not the man you were when you were young. And wherever she is today, Leonora surely must have changed, too. Am I not right, my friend?"

"Maybe, maybe not," Sergio answered. "But you are right. That's why I wanted to see you this morning, to show you this." He reached inside his jacket pocket and retrieved two small photos. "Remember when you first saw these?" He handed Paolo the photos.

Paolo shook his head slowly. He couldn't believe Sergio still had these faded snapshots of a girl who had left him in the dust years ago.

"Forget her," was all Paolo said. He leaned back in his chair and closed his eyes. He could be home preparing breakfast for the twins. Anna was down with morning sickness. He had all day to ready himself for tonight's Haunted Venice walking tour, yet here he was, early in the morning, looking at faded photographs of someone he'd never met.

Sergio took a deep breath. He was losing Paolo's attention. It was now or never, and he could only hope his friend didn't think he was crazy for coming up with such a story.

"Leonora has a twin, " he blurted. "Her twin is here."

Paolo's eyes flew open. He came to attention as would a soldier at roll call.

"Where do you mean 'here'? In Italy? In Venice? How do you know? Is it a twin sister or a twin brother? You never told me Leonora had any siblings, let alone a twin!"

Sergio shook his head. "No no no, Paolo, you misunderstand. Leonora's twin is a woman, but she never lived in Venice. And she isn't related to Leonora. She is a twin in *appearance*, a 'double' as they say. She is identical to, what I mean is, how can I…" Sergio grasped for a comparison.

Paolo had never heard his friend so tongue tied. "As in identical right down to a strand of hair?" he prompted.

Sergio beamed. "Vero! True! To a strand of hair!" Sergio made a fist and slapped the table with his knuckles like a judge lowering a gavel.

"Go on," Paolo said, scrutinizing the photos. The old photos showed a teenaged Leonora Santella. *How old is the so-called double?* Paolo asked himself.

Sergio was on his feet now. "I tell you, Paolo, she came out of nowhere, sat right here in my café, then she disappeared into the crowd. She comes and goes like a dream in the night."

Paolo looked up from the photos and nodded slowly. Sergio was making sense now. "Ah! I get it! This lookalike girl, she's an illusion then. You imagined her in a daydream. And she was as real as the real Leonora Santella. You always have fantasies when it comes to women, my friend and you have always wanted the women who are impossibly out of reach. Then you place those fantasies in your world. You make the women you are actually dating, into the women who are so hard to get! Remember when you were going out with Maralina Marcoli and you introduced her to me as Maralina *Monroe*?"

Sergio shuddered. "Don't remind me. I want to forget

how I made such a fool of myself. But Maralina did look like that famous American actress. You know, with all that gorgeous platinum blonde hair and full lips."

Paolo laughed. "But the *real* Marilyn Monroe had passed away decades before you even met Maralina. Did you think that Marilyn Monroe had reincarnated?"

Sergio waved off Paolo's remark. "But that was then. I was young and impressionable."

Paolo snorted. He laid the photographs face down on the table. "And what are you now, my friend? Do you not see how this so-called 'double' of your first love has made such an impression on you? And I take it you haven't even met her! Is that why you wanted to talk to me? What do you want *me* to do about that?"

Sergio took a third photo out of his jacket pocket. He placed it face up on the table on top of the photos of Leonora. This photo included himself and Leonora, together in the Dorsoduro Sestiere, on her nineteenth birthday. They had gone with some friends to the Guggenheim, then to the Cathedral of Santa Maria della Salute to pose for a picture. The Cathedral would have been where they would marry someday, Sergio reflected as he waited for Paolo to comment on the image. Sergio had not gone into the Cathedral again since that day, though he knew it was still beautiful, holding a timeless beauty with its marbled statuary and dome. It was especially lovely at dusk in silhouette against a setting Venetian sun. The Cathedral possessed a timeless beauty, just as be believed Leonora had, and just as he knew her double also possessed. But Sergio knew that he didn't have the luxury of time. The tall, lovely stranger was only touring Venice for a short time. She'd leave soon, just as Leonora had left.

Paolo spoke, "I have not seen this photograph before." He picked it up and examined it as if it were under a microscope. As he listened to Sergio recount the day and the reason for his and Leonora posing before the beautiful Cathedral, he wondered if his friend's young love had stayed, would she have been willing to stick by Sergio even through tough times, and if Sergio would have been able to do likewise. Would they have withstood the test of time as steadfastly as did the Cathedral of Santa Maria della Salute?

He returned the photo to the table, but did not reject the image as one of a man trying to capture the past and make it part of the present.

"I know of your Leonora," Paolo reiterated. "But this is the first time she is a real person in relation to you. This is the first time I am seeing the both of you in one place, embracing and happy. She is not an illusion."

"Of course she isn't!" Sergio exclaimed. He gathered all of the photos and returned them to his pocket. "And what I want you to do about it, as you put it, is to please, please think hard about last evening. Didn't you see her? The lady who looks just like my Leonora? I'm sure you must remember at least a few faces in your audience. Or at least Giacomo Casanova would remember if not Paolo Trezzi!"

A long silence fell between the two friends until a waiter brought more espresso to the table along with the biscotti, part of the bet Paolo and Sergio had made. Paolo took a biscotti from the platter. He ate slowly, as if mentally retracing his steps from the night before with each bite. After a minute, he shook his head. "I'm sorry, I don't remember."

"She was with two people, a shorter woman, with short hair, and a man. He was tall, like her. You shook hands with him and you kissed the ladies' hands."

Paolo chuckled. "I always kiss the ladies' hands. And

as I remember now, there *was* a small group of three among the tourists. They stuck together and didn't mingle with the others. The ladies appeared to be watching over this man, almost as if they were afraid he'd fly off somewhere. He seemed very interested in the performance."

"And the tall lady with him, tell me what you thought of her," Sergio urged his friend.

"Yes, she was tall," Paolo said. "I thought I had seen her somewhere, but I could not come up with a time or place. It was just a fleeting hunch. But I'm sure I was mistaken. I see so many tourists in my line of work, Sergio. After a while they become a blur. But yes, I remember that group of three."

Sergio again brought out his pocket of photos and placed them all on the table. "Look again, Paolo. Please. You had a hunch, you say, about the tall lady. This is more than what you had a half hour ago. Think harder."

Paolo checked his watch. Anna would be wondering where he was. With his in-laws coming into town tomorrow for a week-long visit, Paolo had promised his wife he'd help convert a spare room from a catch-all space to something resembling a guest room. He imagined his beautiful, usually patient Anna wringing her hands with worry as to what was keeping him so long at the Caffe La Rosa. He'd told her that he'd made a small bet with Sergio and was collecting his winnings this morning. How he'd explain to Anna that the small bet was for espresso and biscotti and not a money bet, he didn't know, but, he was sure she wouldn't mind what he won as long as he would work some magic on turning their catch-all room into comfortable sleeping quarters for her parents.

Paolo looked one last time at each of the three photos, then handed them back to his friend. "I cannot say. I see so many tourists. Our city is swarming with them, not that I mind, of course. They help me make a living. But who can remember every face?" Paolo sighed. "I'm sorry, Sergio. Is this what you wanted to see me about? To show me this photo again? I still don't see the connection…"

Sergio knew he was being too hard on his friend. "Okay. Enough of this. Sorry I kept going on about it, Paolo." He returned the photos to his jacket pocket. "Let me get some biscotti from the kitchen to send home with you. You showed up as promised."

Paolo nodded. "Friends do that for friends. And you don't need to send me home with biscotti. Anna is going to be baking her head off for her parents. I have to go shopping tomorrow morning for her, too. And I have to move furniture today."

Sergio raised his eyebrows.

"Don't ask." Paolo grinned. "When you get married, you marry the whole family, not just the ones you and your spouse add to it." He slapped his knee good naturedly, and pulled back from his chair. "Got to go, my friend. Is there anything I can do for you?"

"Yes," Sergio replied, smiling now. "Please give your beautiful wife and the twins kisses for me. And congratulations again! I meant to ask you last night. Will you be having a boy or a girl, do you know?"

"We don't know, but to be blessed with a bambina, a baby girl, that would be great!" Paolo replied, beaming. "Anna and I always wanted one or two of both! If it is a girl, she will be Rita."

"And if it is another boy?" Sergio asked.

"He will be Sergio!" Paolo exclaimed. "After you! You are going to be the Godfather, yes? You have not changed your mind since last night, I hope."

"Not a chance!" Sergio exclaimed. "I am very happy to be Godfather to baby Trezzi, boy or girl! Rita is a beautiful name! And if it is a boy, I am honored that you and Anna wish to name him for me."

The two friends shook hands warmly. "Mille grazie!" Paolo said.

"Oh, by the way," he added, "Gloria Bartolo is going to be the Godmother. You remember Gloria, yes?"

"I do," Sergio replied. "Isn't Gloria one of Anna's older sisters, the one with the five children?"

Paolo started counting on his fingers. He gave a low whistle. "Mamma Mia! How fast the time goes by! Gloria and Umberto have *seven* kids now."

Sergio whistled back. "They sure keep busy!"

Paolo laughed heartily. "Like the saying goes 'time passes quickly, so strike while the iron is hot'!" He became serious then. "Anna and I are not kids anymore. We have to do just that, strike. Now or never. We married late, in our thirties. And we are thrilled that our Antonio and Francesco are going to have another playmate, and that we're still not too over the hill to make it happen."

Sergio didn't think Paolo and Anna were over the hill by any stretch of the imagination. Still, he couldn't help himself from making light of his friend's point of view.

"Nothing like reaching the finish line just under the wire, yes? he joked.

"Who's finished? Paolo countered, grinning as he got up from his chair. "We're just getting started! " He glanced at his watch again. "Whoa! I'm in trouble now! I have to get going. Are you cool?"

"I'm cool," Sergio assured his friend. "I'll walk with you to the fondamenta."

"Good, 'cause I have a couple of jokes to tell you about my mother-in-law's cooking," Paolo said.

"Is she a lousy cook?" Sergio asked.

Paolo winked. "Just use somebody else's name if you re-tell the jokes okay?"

Returning to Caffe La Rosa, Sergio felt better than ever. Even though Paolo hadn't been able to confirm that the tall woman at the *Haunted Venice* tour was indisputably Leonora's lookalike twin, Sergio was sure that he was on to something good. Having been asked to serve as Godfather to Paolo and Anna's third child had made Sergio suddenly feel he had something exciting to look forward to besides working by day, filling his dance card by night, and, more recently, imagining Leonora was back, if only in the form and fashion of a tourist bearing a remarkable likeness to his lost love.

Wherever his Leonora was tonight, it was none of his concern. As for the tall, lovely stranger, if she visited his café again, he would make a point of approaching her. He would introduce himself. Ideally, she would return an introduction. He would learn her name, her real name. She would be who she was, not a double, not a "twin" or a reincarnation, in short, not Leonora Santella. He would make some conversation with her, if time allowed and, if time didn't allow, he'd do what Paolo would do: *strike while the iron is hot*.

Chapter 6

Elaine and Carol sat in the hotel lobby, waiting for Randy
to surface. Earlier that morning, he'd gone with Carol on
a fresh-fruit hunt. They'd walked to Via Garibaldi to
check out a spot the hotel concierge had enthusiastically
endorsed: a produce barge docked at the far end of the
Via. After last evening's Haunted Venice tour, Randy and
his sisters had enjoyed larger than sensible helpings of
dolce after dinner. A gelato stand, open late, completed
the evening's calories binge. The threesome put away
several containers of the delectable Italian version of ice
cream while sitting around the television watching
movies.

To Randy's great relief, the films had come with
English subtitles, but that had been the extent of any
relief he'd feel for a while. A wave of heartburn hit him
in the middle of the night. As he tossed, turned and
belched the hours away, Randy knew he'd overdone it
with the desserts. *I'll eat better tomorrow*, he promised
himself before finally falling back to sleep. A tapping at
his door at just after sun-up turned out to be Carol,
announcing her plans to make an early morning trip to

Via Garibaldi for provisions to store in their connecting rooms' mini fridges. Did Randy want something in particular? First he said no, then suddenly added, "Wait, I'll come with you!" Fresh fruit sounded sensible compared to last night's gelato gorge.

Carol had returned to the hotel an hour later, produce in arms, but without Randy.

"Where did you lose him?" Elaine asked between bites of one of the fresh peaches Carol had brought back. It was so sweet and juicy that Elaine had to hold one hand under her chin while she ate, to keep the peach nectar from escaping onto her summer slacks. Elaine could have used a sink right now. And where to dispose of the peach pit? Carol wanted to wait downstairs for their brother. Elaine had taken her peach breakfast "to go" and joined her in the lobby. Now Elaine looked around to see if anyone noticed her licking her fingers.

Carol was talking. "I didn't lose him, he took off. Here, sis. Don't make a mess." She pulled a tissue from her pocket and offered it to Elaine.

Elaine hesitated. "Did you…"

"Of course not!" Carol huffed, placing the tissue on Elaines lap. "I don't recycle tissues!"

Elaine was a germophobe. She often told Carol that she'd never be able to do what Carol did every day as an ER nurse. As close as the two sisters were, they were far apart in some ways, not just in appearance. They had different temperaments, different tastes, even different levels of luck in love, Elaine being the more blessed in the love department. This morning, in fact, Elaine had confessed waking up to an impossible urge. She just had to see Albert in person. No Zoom app meets. No Facetime. She wanted her husband by her side *for real.* How to do that from opposite sides of the world? Elaine had confided to Carol about her sudden urge to be with Albert. As they shared a blow dryer, elbowing each other before the mirror, Elaine had pondered out loud if last evening's Casanova experience might have caused her sudden urge to be with her husband. What she'd kept to herself, though, was how she felt about staying in Venice for the full two weeks of their planned vacation. She hadn't anticipated missing Albert this much, but Elaine knew better than to tell Carol that she would rather be home than here in a Venetian hotel with a six-hour time difference separating her from her husband. *Now here I am with my sister eating fruit in a hotel lobby on the other side of the world, waiting for our kid brother to resurface.*

Another giggle bubbled up inside of Elaine. She thought of Randy, tall and lanky in construction boots, wearing his tool belt, but sitting in a baby stroller. With Carol pushing it.

Carol was staring at her. "What's so funny?"

Elaine shook her head as she wrapped the peach pit in the tissue. "Nothing, really. I was just thinking, sis, do you believe in fate?"

Carol frowned. "Fate? Do you mean like, something happens because it's supposed to, and there's nothing you can do about it? Or do you mean something like luck, the roll of the dice? Right place right time?"

Elaine shrugged. "I don't know, maybe both. Or maybe *right* place but *wrong* time…"

"I believe in luck, good and bad," Carol replied. "Fate, I don't know. Why?"

Elaine stood up. She scanned the lobby. "Never mind, sis. Listen. I'm going to go back to the room and wash up. My hands are so sticky. And I need to lose this peach pit. I don't see a waste receptacle anywhere in this lobby and I'm not dumping it in an ashtray in the smoking section."

Carol laughed. "Like our brother would do! Go on upstairs. I'm going to wait for Randy outside." She stretched her long legs in front of her. "Wow, I'm getting a tan already."

"Yes, I see that," Elaine acknowledged. "And we haven't even been to Lido Beach yet!"

Carol drew in a breath and slowly exhaled. Elaine had a point. Randy is holding us up, she said to herself.

"Can you take the rest of this produce upstairs?" Carol asked.

Elaine took the large bag of fruit into her arms. "My turn to be the beast of burden, " Elaine joked. "See you outside."

At the elevator, Elaine watched the arrow above the door move with each descending stop. When the elevator reached the lobby, its doors opened to a car empty but for a single passenger, a military man in dressed in United States Army uniform fatigues and carrying a duffle bag over his shoulders. He nodded politely to Elaine.

"Thank you for your service," Elaine offered. It was an acknowledgment often extended to servicemen and women, not just during official military holidays, but everyday, anywhere.

The soldier nodded again and surprised Elaine by offering her a quick salute. "Thank you, ma'am," he said as he passed and walked briskly to the concierge desk.

Stepping into the elevator car, Elaine turned and caught a last glimpse of the soldier. Before the elevator doors closed, she heard the concierge wish the soldier a safe trip.

Elaine thought of her husband. Albert Page had an ear for sound. A music major in college, he nonetheless yearned for a career in the military. Right out of college, he'd applied to the United States Navy SEAL program, but the Navy rejected him. His ears were perfect, but his vision wasn't. He was diagnosed with protanomaly, a form of red/green colorblindness. Even the customized eyewear that allowed him to perform color-related tasks much easier did not help his chances of making it into the SEAL program. Albert had told her often that, with hindsight, he saw that the Navy's decision not to allow him a waiver for his condition was the best thing that had ever happened to him. Albert had taken the Navy's decision hard at first, but a year later, he met Elaine. If he'd been a SEAL, he'd reasoned, they may never have met. Elaine herself often reflected on what her life might have looked like being married to a SEAL. The thought of perhaps ending up a young widow scared her, as SEAL teams were always sent to do the most dangerous work. She was happy being the wife of a recording studio backup musician who, for relaxation, enjoyed nothing more than binge watching military action movies with Papa Bear at his feet.

As she exited the elevator at her floor, Elaine wondered if Albert was thinking of her this moment, as she was thinking of him. Had he eaten breakfast yet? No, it would be too early for him to be up, let alone having breakfast. When her husband did wake up and put on the coffee, toast an English muffin, spreading on strawberry preserves—his favorite topping because Elaine put up the preserves herself—would he suddenly miss her terribly, so terribly that it hurt?

Entering her room, Elaine disposed of the sticky wad of tissue and peach pit and went into the bathroom to wash her hands. She wondered about the soldier. Did he have family waiting? Was there someone at home preparing a feast to celebrate his safe return? Had they missed him so much that it hurt?

A knock at the door interrupted Elaine's thoughts. She quickly rinsed and dried her hands.

"Carol? Randy?" she called as she approached the door.

"Room service!" a squeaky, high-pitched voice answered. Elaine knotted her brow.

"Sorry, I didn't order room service," she answered from inside her room. She held the doorknob but didn't turn it. If she weren't so short, she could reach the security peephole. As it was, the best she could do was to try to decipher the voice.

Silence on the other side of the door. Then, the squeaky, high-pitched voice repeated, "Room service!"

Elaine raised her voice. "I told you I did not order. You must have the wrong room."

The voice persisted. "Room service! You must open pronto quick-o!"

Quick-o? As in *Sigg-nor?* Elaine fixed her best smirk as she turned the doorknob. Randy had to be the one on the other side of the door, playing a joke. Carol had lost him, and this was probably why. Is was the best he could do with time on his hands.

"Ever the comedian," Elaine muttered as she opened

the door. Before she could say another word, a profusion of color surrounded her. The bouquet, abundant with fragrant lilacs, roses, carnations, delicate fronds and baby's breath bouquet, was mixed with the familiar woodsy scent of cedar infused with spice.

Albert's favorite cologne.

Chapter 7

The couple chose the table that interrupted Sergio's view of the pedestrian traffic entering the Via Garibaldi from the Riva degli Schiavoni. Sergio made a mental note to speak to his wait staff. Perhaps something could be arranged to see that, when Sergio was seated at his usual spot at the café's indoor entrance, the outdoor tables could be slightly rearranged so that he would not have to crane his neck to catch the street action. He dismissed the notion seconds later. His café was busy, especially in the mid-mornings. His staff hardly had time to take their scheduled breaks let alone redesign the layout of the outdoor seating. Besides, tourists were important at this time of year, and the couple blocking his view were definitely tourists. He could tell by the enormous sun visor worn by the woman at the table. He'd noticed over the years that foreign tourists seemed to wear those oversized visors more so than the locals. They were sold all over the city, but Sergio rarely saw a local wearing one. A shop owner he knew who sold mainly sundries and last-minute needs like aspirin or hair combs, once told him that, if it weren't for tourists' demands, he'd eliminate half of his inventory. Still, what the tourists wanted, Venice's businesses supplied. Where the tourists wanted to sit, they would sit. *Venice is not in a hurry*, Sergio reminded himself. People can take their time here. And at his café, the tourists could stay as long as they'd like and sit wherever they wanted, just like the locals did, unless there was a very good reason limiting this flexibility. Sergio remembered an instance several years ago, when more than the usual number of pigeons swarmed the buildings on the Via Garibaldi, competing with the sea gulls for scraps. Even table umbrellas and awnings couldn't keep the birds, or their droppings, away from the café patrons! A smile escaped him in spite of the seriousness of that long-past occurrence. With poise and promptness, and always, always putting the customer first, Sergio and his staff had repositioned the tables away from the ledges and outcroppings, with hardly a wrinkle in the pace and quality of the service.

Sergio leaned to one side of his table and stretched his neck again to get a better view of the Via. Perhaps he could change his own seat without anyone noticing, he thought. But no, it was better to remain in the background, especially since he was the proprietor. He didn't want his customers to know he was watching them, hoping that one of them would be Leonora's lookalike, returning to the café, perhaps looking for him. He was sure she had glanced at him with a hint of recognition when they were both on the *Haunted Venice* walking tour. Still, with no guarantees, Sergio could only watch and wait and hope that the lovely stranger would walk his way today. He knew she was still in the city. Just this morning Paolo had sent him a text message this morning.

The lady who you call Leonora's twin was with the young guy buying fruit. I saw them yesterday.

Rather than text back, Sergio called his friend. "What are you doing up this early?"

Paolo reminded him of his in-laws' visit. "I had to go to the produce barge first thing for avocados. Anna's mother eats them for breakfast. Can you believe it? Why won't an orange do? But for my Anna, I will go broke to feed her mother." Paolo's hearty laugh hit Sergio like an energy drink. His friend's upbeat optimism in the face of a picky mother-in-law, fueled by his love for his wife, left Sergio feeling upbeat and optimistic as well, so much so that he decided to open up at Caffe La Rosa earlier than usual. Sergio also decided that, today, he would dress up as if it were evening. He would choose a silk tie from his wardrobe, rather than going open collared. He would also wear his black leather laced shoes, shined to a high buff, rather than his casual loafers. And, for a change, Sergio decided to walk to work this morning rather than board a vaporetto and wait all day at his café if that was what it would take to see the tall, lovely lady again. *Keep upbeat and optimistic*, Sergio repeated to himself as he whistled softly.

The sun was up already, and there was no breeze off the Grand Canal. The waters were still, save for a few early morning craft. It would be hot today, Sergio predicted. Still, he would keep his silk tie neatly knotted and his shoes securely tied. If he saw the lady again, Sergio decided, he would approach her and introduce himself. He tried not to overthink the possible outcomes of taking an initiative like this, but it was difficult not to imagine both the best and worst scenarios. At best, he would finally learn her name if she returned his introduction. At worst, he would return home having not seen her at all and, if this were to be the outcome, so be it. He'd just try again tomorrow, and the next day, and the next after that, for as long as he knew she was still in Venice.

What Sergio hadn't expected after opening up early and settling in at his private table, was seeing double.

Another mega-brimmed, neon pink sun visor, identical to the one blocking his view was bobbing its way toward his café. Sergio shifted his chair to get a better view just as Fernando, one of his waiters, approached him, nervously clicking his pen as he spoke.

"Remember that group of tourists I you about, with the two ladies and the younger man who wanted to buy everybody drinks and didn't have any Euros?"

"I remember well," Sergio nodded to Fernando. "You called them 'homeless' and I didn't understand what you meant. I'm still not clear about that. What did you mean?"

Fernando blinked. "You don't see it? The bags! They had so many bags all stuffed under the table, they were either shoplifters or homeless. That's all I can say."

"So, is there a problem?" asked Sergio.

"They're back," Fernando replied, pointing to the table where, now, identical sun visors were vying for space while the women beneath them exchanged the traditional European kiss on each cheek greeting.

"But the man with no money isn't with them now," Fernando added.

"Ah," was all Sergio answered. He was only half listening to Fernando. At last, one of the sun visors, removed by its wearer, was relegated to the table top. Sergio relaxed his neck and shoulders and settled back in his chair. His view was much better now.

Chapter 8

Carol waved off her brother-in-law's gesture. "Thanks, Albert, I'd sit if I had time, but I'm on my way to mail these." She held out a stack of post cards. "I wrote them out last night while you and Elaine were *busy*." Carol stifled a giggle.

Elaine's sun visor concealed a rising blush.

Albert had so missed being away from Elaine, to the point where he had felt it was only right to apologize to Elaine and Carol for his adding yet another guy to their original "just us gals" vacation plan.

Carol accepted his apology, though she didn't think he needed to give one. "You are always welcome to crash a party, Al!" she joked. She was glad he showed up the day before yesterday, for Elaine's sake. As for Elaine, her husband's surprise arrival was nothing short of a godsend. She had not only missed him like crazy, but she needed a new personal porter.

Elaine sensed that Randy had grown weary being around his sisters almost every hour of the day since they'd arrived in Venice. At any rate, the personal porter job was Albert's if he wanted it, and, to Elaine's relief, he did. Albert's only condition: that he'd start work "after my bride and I make up for lost time". Elaine couldn't complain! She moved in with Albert to the hotel's Honeymoon Suite.

To speed up the honeymoon, Carol had repacked Elaine's things and had the suitcases and tote bags transported to the honeymooners' love nest. She then returned to the lobby and continued a vigil for two hours, moving between the hotel lobby and the wide expanse of the Riva degli Schiavoni, the waterfront walkway where everything and everyone could eventually be found strolling if they weren't at Piazza San Marco or on the Via Garibaldi. That night passed with no word from Randy. Carol didn't call Elaine and Al. She wasn't about to interrupt the honeymoon.

Yesterday, a boxed gift had arrived for Carol, along with a room service cart of coffee and pastries. Elaine's generosity warmed Carol's heart, especially as she read the note the hotel steward presented her as he wheeled in the surprise goodies. Carol recognized Elaine's neatly scripted handwriting immediately.

Supersized sun visors! One for you and one for me! Albert's treat! Your breakfast, MY treat!

Carol appreciated the surprises. Still, between Randy taking off to who knew where, and Elaine moving out of their shared room, Carol felt like she was walking on shifting sand. Randy still hadn't surfaced. Carol checked yet again with the doormen, the concierge, the porters, the servers from the Floating Patio restaurant, the bartender, even the chamber maids. Not one had seen or heard from her brother.

Yesterday afternoon, Carol took one more walk along the Riva, exploring each quay, each fondamenta, between their hotel and the Doge Palace. On the way, she stopped at a shop that sold postcards and stamps, bought one card of each scene pictured on the display rack, and a sheet of international stamps. *There, now I have something to do besides drive myself crazy.* Later, in her room, Carol wrote out her cards. She could leave them with the desk to post, but decided not to go down to the lobby again. She was even too tired to eat. Worrying about her brother exhausted her. If Randy hadn't returned by tomorrow, Carol decided, she would report him missing. By then it would be three whole days since he'd disappeared from the produce barge on the Via Garibaldi.

When a knock on the door of the connecting room

woke her out of a fitful sleep, Carol bolted across the room and unlatched the door to find not only Randy, but a petite, curly-haired blue-eyed blonde on his arm. The girl sported a *Princeton University* tee shirt over a denim skirt that looked like it had seen better days. On her feet, she wore rubber flip flops. She introduced herself as Vicky Potts, "from Lambertville *and* Princeton, New Jersey." She ran a finger across the printed words on her tee.

"But she's only in Venice because her parents think she needs enrichment," Randy added.

Poor girl is in need of a wardrobe, Carol thought. As for her brother, wherever he had been off to for the past three days, he looked no worse for wear. Carol was so relieved to have him back at the hotel, she only half listened to his banter about how Vicky had found him, lost and with limited Italian language skills, trying to find his way back to his family. What Carol really wanted then was to get a peaceful, worry-free night's sleep.

***

Carol had hoped to fill Elaine and Albert in on Randy's middle of the night return, but was now the right time? Clearly, her sister and brother-in-law were continuing their honeymoon on the Via Garibaldi this morning, and Carol didn't want to get in the way.

"Sure you won't stay and have some refreshment with us?" Elaine prodded.

Carol shook her head, the wide-brim visor competing with her hands for space as she held out her post cards. "I'd like to, but I'm not about to crash a honeymoon." She flipped through her post cards. "And I want to get to a mailbox as soon as possible so the cards can get home before I do."

Elaine pulled off her sun visor and placed it on the table. "Wait, sis. Before you go, what's with Randy? When did he finally get back? We saw him this morning with a blonde-haired girl in the lobby. He didn't see us, and we didn't want to interrupt him. He looked stricken, if you want the truth."

Carol frowned. "Stricken?"

"Yep, stricken by Cupid's arrow," Al chimed in. "He was pouring over that girl like maple syrup over hotcakes. And, no wonder!"

"Albert!" Elaine slapped her husband's wrist. "What's that supposed to mean!"

"It means your brother is sweet on a hottie! Get it? " Albert winked.

Carol stifled a giggle.

Elaine shifted in her seat, putting some distance between herself and her husband. "Forgive Al, Carol, he's a wolf lately. His mind's in the gutter. This is the first time I'm sitting upright since he got here."

Carol couldn't hold back a squeal. "Whooooaa! Look whose mind is in the gutter now! You two had better get back to the hotel before you cause a ruckus!"

As quickly as she'd separated herself from Albert, Elaine leaned into him again. "We were so busy last night, we could hardly catch a breath, isn't that true, Al?"

Albert just smiled. It was the smile of a very contented man. Carol remembered Evan wearing the same smile the morning after. What eluded her was any memory of herself feeling similarly contented. At the moment, she was just plain mortified. That sister of hers was sometimes more of a scene maker than Randy was!

"Don't say another word, sis," Carol hissed. She could feel her cheeks growing warm from hearing all this sexy banter. *Boy, do I need a life or what?* she asked herself silently. When was the last time she…? *Never mind, Carol. Never mind.*

Albert spoke up. "We're in *Venice*, it's okay." He pointed to Carol's post cards. "Let me mail those for you. I need to stretch my legs anyway. We've been sitting here for over an hour. Just keep an eye on my bride, don't let any hotshot gondolier steal her away!" He stood up and, with a low bow and a sweep of his arm, invited Carol to keep his seat warm until he got back.

Carol hesitated, then shrugged and settled herself into Albert's chair.

"Thanks, Al. " Carol forced a smile. What she really wanted was to do was return to the hotel as soon as possible and go back to sleep. She needed a full reset. That was the plan, just as soon she found a birthday gift for Albert.

Carol didn't expect to be invited to any celebration her sister might have planned for Albert's birthday. Back home it would be different. Elaine would call up the family and everyone would meet at her and Albert's home and enjoy the traditional birthday party, complete with cake, wish making, and blowing out the candles. But here, no. Venice was simply too romantic for that. Carol was certain her sister and brother-in-law would want to be alone, perhaps celebrating on a gondola ride beneath the famous Bridge of Sighs. When couples kiss beneath that bridge, it is said that they will have happiness ever after together, or some such nonsense Carol didn't believe. If it were true, then why were divorce lawyers so busy? Carol could see that Albert and Elaine were as tight as a married couple could be, even finishing each other's sentences sometimes. She didn't think they'd need to lean on any myths to seal their happily ever after.

Carol tried to stay alert in the increasing heat that seemed stronger today than at any time since they'd arrived in Italy. She closed her eyes briefly and listened to the murmurs of the people at the tables nearby, the clatter of ice against glass, the pop of a wine cork. The sounds were like a voice whispering, relax, don't think, just be.

Elaine touched her elbow and Carol opened her eyes. "Don't conk out on me, sis," Elaine said. "What have you been up to while Al and I were on our spontaneous honeymoon?"

Carol smiled weakly. "Don't remind me of what I'm

missing. Since Evan and I called it quits, I'm like a nun. A nun without a Casanova to sneak into my room and whisk me away to a jazzy honeymoon suite in the night."

Elaine lowered her sunglasses to the tip of her nose. She stared at Carol hard, but her eyes were laughing. Carol broke out in a giggle, Elaine followed suit and in no time the two sisters were transported back to where they'd been before Albert and Randy had interrupted the plans they'd made so long ago.

"Here we are, just us gals!" Elaine chirped.

Carol raised her arms eye level and spread the fingers on her hands. "I need a mani!" she announced.

Elaine stuck a sandaled foot from beneath the table and examined her toes. "And I need a pedi!"

"Let's go, then," Carol said. She felt so much better kicking back with Elaine. This is how she'd envisioned her vacation. "Soon as your hubby gets back, let's tell him we're going to look for a nail salon!"

Elaine smiled as she took off her sunglasses and fiddled with the stems before placing them back on, shielding her eyes. "I can't, I'm sorry sis," she said softly. "I wish I could," she went on. "I mean, we had plans and all, but tomorrow is Al's birthday."

"I know!" Carol said. "I have a gift card waiting at home for him. I figured I'd see him when we got back, but now that he's here…"

Elaine leaned over and hugged Carol so hard that Carol's sun visor tilted sharply to one side of her head. "Honey, you're the best," Elaine whispered.

"Oh I know that." Carol grinned as she removed her sun visor and placed it on the table next to Elaine's.

"What I mean is, it's Albert's birthday tomorrow, as you know, and we've decided to spend it going—"

"I know, I know," Carol interrupted her sister. "You're going off by yourselves, no cake, no candles, just a romantic honeymoon birthday combo deal. That's great! I'll give Al his present before you leave. Are you and Al going to Lido Beach? Just curious. I promise I won't crash your cabana! And I won't text anybody back home and tip them off, either!"

The sisters shared another laugh at the notion that Carol would show up at Lido Beach with a cake, candles, Papa Bear and the entire extended Duncan family.

Carol turned to Elaine. "I may as well tell you now before I take off to look for a gift for your hubby. This girl Randy met, her name is Vicky Potts, she's probably the same girl you saw him with in the lobby. She lives near us, sis. She's from Lambertville. And she goes to school even closer by than that. Princeton."

Elaine pursed her lips. "Hmm, Princeton. Fancy schmancy."

"I have a hunch we'll see her again, and not on this side of the world," Carol said.

"And you think maybe our Randy has a shot in the dark with this girl?" Elaine asked.

"She said *she* found *him*," Carol said.

"Like finding a stray?" Elaine's lips softened into a smile. "Well, he's one lucky stray, if that's how it happened. A Princeton girl. Our Randy always lands on his feet. See? You worry for no reason, sis. He's a survivor."

"That's one way to look at it." It didn't occur to her until now that Elaine hadn't worried half as much about their brother as she had. Then again, Elaine had received the surprise of her life when her husband had shown up in Venice the same day Randy disappeared into the maze of the city. Carol could hardly blame her sister for being more focused on her husband's arrival than on the departure of their brother for parts unknown, and for being found, "like a stray" by a stranger.

"Can you imagine our brother going out with an Ivy Leaguer?" Elaine mused. She tapped her knuckles on the table. "I'm thinking, maybe that's just what Randy needs."

"What do you mean?" asked Carol.

Elaine leaned back in her chair. "We know he's still holding a torch for Joyce. And even coming here with us isn't enough. He needs a new lady, not new scenery."

"I agree one hundred percent," Carol replied. "I just hope Vicky Potts doesn't give him ideas about her Ivy League lifestyle."

"What Ivy League lifestyle, Carol?" Elaine asked. If her sister was anything, Elaine knew, she was impressionable.

Carol shrugged. "I don't know, maybe I'm just idealizing the whole Ivy League thing because *we* never went to schools like Princeton."

No kidding, Elaine thought. How often she'd passed by the Princeton campus wondering how anyone could afford to go there!

"The Duncan family didn't have the money to send their kids to schools like that," Elaine reminded Carol.

"And even scholarships were hard to come by."

"But we had the grades," Carol countered.

"*You* had the grades," Elaine corrected her sister. "But you had your heart set on going to Rutgers, remember? You didn't care about Ivy League."

"I didn't then," Carol replied. "But now, because of Randy and this Vicky Potts, I can't get that school out of my mind. It's so *not* our brother's turf."

Elaine waved to Albert as he approached them. "Randy can handle a Princeton coed. But can *you* handle not worrying about him?"

Before Carol could answer, Albert was back at their table. "Cards are in the mail!" he announced cheerfully.

"Thanks Al. I want to get going now. I have some shopping to do." She and Elaine exchanged knowing glances. Just then, Carol noticed the waiter who served them the morning Randy had caused such a commotion. The waiter hurriedly moved between the tables as he carried plates and cups on a tray. Their eyes met ever so briefly just as Carol picked up her sun visor to put it on. Carol turned to Elaine. "I think that waiter remembers us," she said.

Elaine smirked. "He was afraid of us. We didn't fit his

criteria, I guess."

Like maybe Randy doesn't fit Vicky's criteria, Carol thought silently. There she was again, worrying about Randy. Elaine was right. She had to stop mothering her brother. She'd wasted so much of her vacation time doing that, while Elaine and Albert had been over the moon and back, making up for lost time.

Carol blew kisses to her sister and brother-in-law as she turned onto the Via Garibaldi. Albert and Elaine waved back, and Albert settled himself beside Elaine.

"How did she take it, babe?" he asked.

Elaine removed her sunglasses and turned to her husband, holding his gaze.

"She's going out looking for a birthday present for you," Elaine answered, trying to keep her voice as steady as her focus.

"That's all?"

Elaine lowered her eyes. "You win our bet, Al. I couldn't tell her we're leaving tomorrow. I just didn't have the heart to do it. Drinks are on me."

Chapter 9

It was now or never, Sergio decided, recalling his and Paolo's talk that night at Bibi's. Paolo had advised him to strike while the iron was hot. Everything was hot today. Sergio wiped his brow with a napkin. He felt weary and constrained in his silk necktie and lace-up shoes. At the same time, every impulse in his body was on overdrive. *She* had been there, right in front of him, at the table. As quickly as he'd glimpsed her, he'd lost her in the bustling of the waiters and customers coming and going.

Maybe she'll retrace her steps, Sergio thought. But his gut eschewed such hope. *Strike while the iron is hot, man!*

Sergio bolted from his chair. He signaled Cosimo and Fernando that he was leaving the premises.

"I bet he's meeting a woman," Cosimo said as he watched his boss sprint onto the Via Garibaldi.

"Maybe not," Fernando replied. "Maybe our boss is dreaming."

It hadn't been lost on the waiters that Sergio was preoccupied lately. They'd also noticed that, so far this week, he hadn't once mentioned who he was going to take to his favorite nightclub this weekend coming. Come to think of it, Cosimo ventured, he bet Sergio hadn't even gone nightclubbing last weekend.

What neither waiter knew was that Sergio had given up on the dating scene the moment he'd laid eyes on the beautiful tall lady who, his logic dictated, was not Leonora Santella, though his heart dictated otherwise.

Carol noticed Sergio before he saw her. She'd lingered on the landing of the second floor of a bi-level shop, yielding to some fast-footed teenagers. When she turned to follow them down the stairs, there he was, also making room, as she had, for the youngsters in a rush. The man's unexpected presence startled Carol. She covered her mouth with the back of her hand, feeling a cough building up from her throat. Instead, her throat tightened. She gasped for air. Her eyes filled with tears, blurring her vision. Suddenly, Carol felt her throat muscles loosen, allowing her to release whatever was stuck in her windpipe. Nothing came up. Her throat muscles tightened again. Instinctively she grabbed the collar of her dress. Seconds dragged before she was able to release a deep, guttural cough so loud it seemed to bounce off walls and floors and ceilings and anything else it could touch as it echoed through the stairwell. Carol knew she looked anything but dignified, but at least she was breathing! Her face flushed as she let herself go, swaying to a rolling cough punctuated by hard breath every third or fourth expulsion. Her sun visor and clutch bag slipped from her hand. She groped for them but couldn't find them, her tears still building, flooding her vision, the harsh echo of her relentless coughing continuing its ricochet from narrow walls to ceiling, straight into Sergio Bari's ears.

"Signorina, let me help you." He'd heard her before realizing who she was. What he did realize was that it didn't matter who this lady was, she was in trouble. He scooped up her belongings and in seconds was by her side on the landing, patting and rubbing her back, gently gathering her long hair, bringing it back, away from her face, giving her air. When her coughing subsided, he helped her down the stairs, lowered her to the bottom step and sat with her there. Nobody was trying to climb or descend the shop's stairs. If he was in their way, too bad. They'd have to wait until this poor lady's breathing slowed. Slowly, the color returned to her cheeks. He wiped her face with his handkerchief, adjusted the dreadful sun visor for her, realizing only then that he had found who he was looking for.

He helped her stand, offered her his arm, and told her he would take her wherever she wanted to go.

Carol didn't resist.

***

"You struck while the iron was hot, alright! And you ended up helping her pick out clothes for another man? Unbelievable! Tell me more!"

Sergio smiled and raised his glass to his friend. "Salute, Casanova!"

"Will you see her again?" Paolo asked.

Sergio sipped his vino slowly. "One thing at a time," he told his friend.

Paolo sighed. "Okay, I get it. No more questions about the future. Just keep talking about what already happened."

Sergio was on the fence about whether or not to divulge every detail of the past twenty-four hours. In truth, he was more focused on the next twenty-four. He had an inner steadiness with him all day. The feeling was still with him amid the crowd inside Bibi's, as he and

Paolo nursed glasses of Chianti. Paolo was marking time until it was safe to go upstairs. He was still in his Casanova costume, waiting until his in-laws were asleep so he could get rid of a plate of pasta his mother-in-law had overcooked without hurting her feelings. Sergio would have liked to hear more of Paolo's stories about the perils of dining with his wife's parents. He wasn't in a hurry to put a jinx on his sense of comfort and calm. A peacefulness, unrushed by any urgency to talk about the tall, beautiful American lady, had stayed with him since yesterday. She was his secret, and, at the same time, the reason behind why he wanted to yell at the top of his lungs for all the world to hear that he had met a lady who was too good to be true.

He would tell Paolo some things, Sergio decided. "She is not who I thought she was, Paolo. She is better," he said quietly.

"What do you mean?" asked Paolo.

"This will take long to unpack, are you sure you won't be missed upstairs?"

"I'm good," Paolo assured Sergio. "The pasta will definitely still be in the fridge. I'm ready to pitch it. Believe me, nobody wants second helpings."

Before they'd finished their first glasses of vino at Bibi's he'd given Paolo enough information, he thought, to satisfy his friend's curiosity. He told Paolo about seeing Leonora's twin at his café, sitting with the short, plump lady she had accompanied on the Haunted Venice tour, how both wore gaudy sun visors with huge brims that blocked his view of the street, and about a man being there too, but not the same man who had been on the walking tour with them.

"What else?" Paolo asked each time Sergio stopped to consider what to leave in and what to leave out. Maybe if he stalled Paolo, he could think things out more.

"I think I'm talked out for tonight," he said, checking the time on the wall clock behind the bar. "It's getting late."

Paolo evidently didn't think so. "The night's young, my friend. Do I have to pull your words out of you?" He pulled his Casanova consume leotard at the knees and stretched the fabric. "Mamma mia, I'm sweating in this get-up. Don't make me sweat more. Please. Spill the beans. *Cough* them up if you have to!"

"Okay, okay," Sergio acquiesced. He moved closer to Paolo and put his head down as he spoke. He felt like a sleuth. But Bibi's was mobbed and the din of conversation among the clientele was getting louder by the hour. It was either yell or give off an appearance of someone making a dirty deal of some sort. He cupped a hand to the side of his face, half whispering.

Paolo leaned in. "Go on, give it up."

Sergio nodded. "So then, I followed her to the end of the Via, and I saved her life."

"You saved her *life*?"

Two patrons at the bar looked at each other, then at Paolo.

"Shhh!" Sergio hissed, edging closer to Paolo. "That's when I saved her from falling down the steps when she took a coughing fit on the second floor landing."

"Oh," was all Paolo said.

Sergio bristled. "Oh? Just 'oh'? Who knows? She could have choked or worse. I was meant to be there, don't you see? It was fate."

Paolo spoke up. "No, it was not fate. You could have been there but done nothing. Some people don't like to get involved. You *chose* to help the lady." He eyed his friend's almost empty glass. "More Chianti?"

Sergio placed the palm of his hand over its rim. "No

more for me, thanks."

Paolo was making more sense than he was, and Paolo was the one wearing a leotard in a bar.

"I need a stiff espresso," he told Paolo.

Paolo ignored the remark. "More Chianti, Rocco!" he yelled over the noise of the crowd. As Paolo saw it, any reason to keep Sergio talking meant that he wouldn't have to go upstairs and deal with his mother-in-law's pasta. For an Italian matriarch, the well-meaning, caring and loving elderly woman was nonetheless the worst cook he'd ever known. How his father-in-law so diplomatically consumed such bland-tasting meals for forty-five years had to be driven by his devotion to his wife, literally for better or worse when it came to her seriously lacking skills in the kitchen. His Anna was an excellent cook, but she deferred to her mother's wishes to help her in her kitchen when she visited. Paolo wished that Anna would simply hand her mother the dishwasher soap pods and show her how to insert them into the machine's cannister, set the timing, and wait for the *finished* light to go on. To his increased frustration, his Anna refused to keep her mother from cooking for them. I don't want to hurt her feelings, was his wife's excuse.

Fair enough, Paolo had conceded, not wanting to promote a mother–daughter cat fight. He'd seen enough of that with his own mother and younger sister! Paolo and Anna agreed he would buy something to eat on the way home from performing his nightly Haunted Venice tour and settle in at Bibi's until his in-laws had dozed off in front of the flatscreen. Anna would place a platter of her mother's boring pasta aside "for Paolo" and, once the coast was clear, the feral cats in the rear courtyard would feast. *What a wonderful wife he had, a true partner for better or worse, even when "worse" was her beloved mother's pasta!* Paolo's heart beat faster just thinking of his Anna. He hoped Sergio would find such a woman someday. He nudged Sergio with his elbow. "And *then*?"

Sergio pondered telling Paolo how he'd walked with Leonora's lookalike from one shop to another, leaving the Via Garibaldi, ending up on the Piazza San Marco with its high-end shops, suggesting various items she might consider purchasing for the "new man" he'd learned was her brother-in-law, a man with a birthday coming up. He sighed, reluctantly giving in to Paolo's wish for another toast with yet more wine brought over by Rocco. This time, they toasted Anna.

Why not tell him? What harm will it do? Sergio put down his glass. By now, Paolo appeared close to salivating for want of more juice, and not the kind that came from grapes.

"And then," Sergio echoed his friend. "Well, *before* then, she had gone into that gift shop, at the end of the Via, you know, the one that flooded so often that the owners had to set up most of the merchandise on the second floor?"

Paolo nodded. "It's next to where the produce barges dock."

"That's the one," said Sergio, lowering his voice again. "It's one of the older buildings on Via Garibaldi, it sells everything, snacks, tobacco, gifts, accessories."

"I know," said Paolo, forming a smirk. "I once bought my Anna a scarf there. She liked it, but she still called me *tightwad*."

Sergio burst into laughter, forgetting all about his concern that his conversation with Paolo would be privy to everyone at the bar.

"Casanova, the tightwad!" Sergio grinned. "Who would have thought!"

Paolo was unphased. "Go on, my friend."

"She was there to find a birthday gift for her brother-in-law. It turns out that *he* was the man, the new one. He is the husband of the plump lady, remember her? They are sisters. And the other guy, the first one, that's their brother. I had a hunch they were all related, now I know for certain." Sergio took a longer sip of vino. He was again awash in a sense of total wellbeing, and satisfied that he'd told Paolo enough.

Paolo still had other ideas. "My friend, you keep saying *she* this, *her* that. You didn't ask her name?"

Sergio didn't want to go that far, but he sensed Paolo wasn't going to let this question die on the vine. "Her name is Carol."

"A beautiful name!" Paolo exclaimed. "Sergio and Carol. Yes, the names go well together." Paolo made another toast. "To the love birds!"

Sergio felt the back of his neck grow hot. It was the vino no doubt. Still, he pivoted from encouraging Paolo to make more toasts and did not raise his glass.

"I recommended she try Callini's for the perfect gift," he continued, changing the subject. "I walked with her there. She liked a particular tie, brushed silk. Indigo."

"You chose the tie, yes?" asked Paolo.

"Yes," Sergio lied. He'd never have done such a thing. He'd known Carol less than an hour when they walked into Callini's. He would no sooner choose a gift for her to give to her brother-in-law than expect her to do the same for him if circumstances were reversed. Instead, he and Carol had perused many colors, patterns and fabric types, but the final decision on which tie to giftwrap was hers alone. Sergio, nonetheless, kept the truth to himself. A guy thing. Carol hadn't gone with his private choice, the gray and black pixel patterned. In fact, she'd made a face when she saw it. *Don't take it personally*, he'd cautioned himself. He noticed how comfortable Carol was, picking out men's ties and wondered why this was so. Had she once been married? Was she married now? Was she in love? Sergio had asked himself these questions last evening as he lay awake in his bed, going over the events of the day, events that prickled his arms like a rash. He was uncomfortably comfortable, unexcitedly worked up, nothing made sense, everything felt great, everything felt weird. Carol. Carol Duncan. She'd gotten to him, alright. And now, Paolo had him on the witness stand. And who's fault was that? Sergio had only himself to point to. As much as he wanted to keep quiet for now, where had he gone? To Casanova! Now the games were beginning, whether or not Sergio was ready and willing to play.

Chapter 10

The phone rang just as Carol prepared to leave her room. Her first thought was to let it ring. Carol wanted to catch Elaine to deliver the tie she'd purchased yesterday for Albert, before they left Venice for a weekend in Padova, Albert's favorite Italian city.

Elaine had sent Carol a text the night before, revealing her plans to convince Albert to take the train to Padova with her "to shop", when in fact, she had purchased two tickets to attend a concert by OPV, the acclaimed Orchestra of Padova and the Veneto. Carol wanted her gift to be part of the celebration, too, even if she couldn't be there.

She noticed the light on the telephone console indicating the call was coming in from the concierge. Why would the concierge be calling? Intrigued, she picked up. There was an envelope for her, the concierge relayed. Did she wish it to be delivered to her room or left with the desk attendant for pick up at her convenience?

"I'll be right down," Carol said.

She hung up the phone and placed Albert's gift box on

the night stand. Hadn't the nice man, Sergio Bari, who had helped her yesterday, told her he'd be in touch? Who else would deliver a note? Randy? Ha! Carol rolled her eyes at the very thought of her brother checking in with her on a daily basis. Hadn't he disappeared for three days only to resurface and disappear again?

No, it had to be Sergio Bari. Carol's hands trembled as she shut the door behind her and trotted down the hall to the elevator which was opening as she approached. Good timing. She'd make quick work of picking up the envelope then grab the elevator again to the Honeymoon Suite to deliver Albert's gift before he and Elaine left for Padova.

In the elevator, she realized her hands were empty save for her room key. She'd left Albert's gift in her room. Carol took a deep breath. Her brain was in overdrive. *Slow down*, she told herself. *Read your message. Go back to the room. Fetch Al's gift. Take it to the Honeymoon Suite. One thing at a time.*

The concierge was waiting for her, envelope in hand. Thanking him, Carol took a seat in the lobby. *One thing at a time*, she reminded herself as she opened the envelope with trembling hands. Her trembling was quickly replaced by a smile so wide she thought her cheeks would burst. The note, handwritten on *Caffe La Rosa* business letterhead was short, sweet, and to the point:

Dear Carol,

Hello again! I will be at your hotel's Floating Patio at eight o'clock tomorrow evening. Please join me for dinner if you are able. I so look forward to seeing you.

Yours,

Sergio

Sergio's note swept her back to their walk along the Riva degli Schiavoni.

After gift shopping at Callini's, Sergio had suggested they stop for some gelato at one of the stands set up on the Riva degli Schiavoni. Carol had happily agreed. Not only was gelato one of her favorite Italian treats, it was especially kind, she thought, of this nice gentleman to take even more time out of his day for her than he already had. Besides, she deserved the diversion, given Elaine and Albert had each other for company, and Randy had Vicky for company now. Why shouldn't she have someone to spend time with too?

It occurred to Carol, as she and Sergio settled themselves comfortably on the low fondamenta and dangled their legs above the water of the Grand Canal, that this was the first time she'd actually socialized with someone other than family since arriving here. As she and Sergio ate their cones, they talked as though they'd known each other for years. What had surprised Carol more than anything was how she hadn't for a second compared Sergio to Evan, nor to any of her beaus before Evan. Sergio Bari was definitely in a class by himself. Yet, there was something about him, Carol felt, that told her he did not see her the same way. She'd brushed the notion aside, and they finished their gelato and continued to her hotel. When they parted company there, he had invited her to return to his café anytime, "for espresso on the house", and to talk with her some more, if she had time, before she returned to America. But a dinner invitation? Carol hadn't expected that.

Of course she'd meet him! But first she had to get to a beauty salon. That monstrosity of a sun visor had flattened her hair, and her nails needed a fresh coat of pastel pink polish. Returning to the elevator, Carol made a mental note to find a hairdresser and a manicurist first thing tomorrow morning. She pressed the elevator button to the top floor. It wasn't until she got off at Albert and Elaine's floor that she again realized she still didn't have Albert's gift with her. She shook her head and groaned. Alone in the elevator, riding down to her floor, she chided herself. *What's wrong with you, Carol?* She suspected she knew the answer, but she wasn't about to shout out to the world how the unexpected generosity of Sergio Bari had made her feel like a magic wand had been waved around her.

***

It would have been bad luck, Sergio thought, to reveal to Paolo that, not only had he invited Carol Duncan to dinner by way of a note left with the concierge at her hotel, but that he held a strong belief that Carol would indeed show up at the Floating Patio at eight o'clock tomorrow evening. Walking home from Bibi's, Sergio was tempted to plan the evening the way he wanted it to unfold. It was hard not to fantasize how time with Carol Duncan could stretch into something much more than simply sharing dinner and conversation.

Better to not put the cart before the horse, he said to himself as he turned into the alley leading to his flat. Still, he had a feeling that perhaps Carol Duncan would be happy to extend their evening *if* he could get her into the Libreria Acqua Alta, one of the places she told him she'd tried to visit only to be met with a shuttered door and an unsettling sense of being watched. He'd sympathized with Carol. He loved the Libreria Acqua Alta, he told her, and wished they could browse the shelves while she was in Venice. Her smile in response had hit him like a breath of fresh air. When was the last time one of his nightclub dates ever included talk of literature let alone having an interest in spending time in a bookshop, *any* bookshop?

If Libreria Acqua Alta weren't in such sorry condition from the last time it flooded, if it were safe to enter the shop before the contractors finished repairing the floors, if all the books were returned to the shelves, if the popular bathtub was reinstalled, of course he would be able to get Carol inside. After all, he practically owned the place.

Chapter 11

Carol dressed for dinner slowly, taking care not to muss her new upswept hairdo or chip her freshly polished nails on the metal clasps of her double string of faux pearls. She would have liked to borrow Elaine's real pearls, but Elaine was gone. So was Albert. But not to Padova.

While she was under the hair dryer at the beauty salon this afternoon, a text came in from Randy. It was the first time she'd heard from her brother since he and Vicky had taken off again: *Al called, they R going back to NJ, sis will text or call U later*. Later, at least as of right now, hadn't materialized yet. There were no calls or texts on Carol's phone from her sister.

My family is evaporating, Carol thought as she continued preparing for her dinner date with Sergio. She didn't know whether to believe her brother or not. Could he just be playing a silly game with her? Carol wanted to believe this, but no, Randy wouldn't make up something like this.

She couldn't deny that they'd *all* been hard to pin down in recent days. Elaine and Al had been in a world of their own. Randy had found a new friend, maybe even more than a friend. As for herself, Carol conceded she wasn't exactly predictable either. She'd gone shopping for a gift on the Via Garibaldi and ended up spending the day with Sergio Bari, a day that had passed so beautifully, but too quickly. They had talked about so many things, shared their likes and interests, discussing music for one thing. Carol had learned how Sergio loved any popular tune he could dance to, which was quite a contrast to her love of opera and ballads, and having two left feet on a dance floor. Neither had the slightest interest in politics. How refreshing was that! They'd also shared bits and pieces of their family trees. Yes, Carol said, she and Randy and Elaine were brother and sisters, but Elaine got their mom's short, plump stature, while she and Randy were "tall drinks of water" like their dad. Sergio divulged his bucket list to Carol, that consisted of only one "must": he wanted to go to the United States to see a World Series baseball game in person, no matter which two teams were competing!

Carol, had a *Venetian* bucket list, she told Sergio, "I want to take a gondola ride at midnight. And, I want to visit the Libreria Acqua Alta. It's been closed since I got here."

Sergio had lowered his eyes ever so briefly when she'd told him this, then seemingly out of nowhere he'd asked her if she'd like to have some gelato. Yet another hour had flown by. Carol had missed her family's comings and goings by a heartbeat that day. She checked the time. Seven thirty-five. She'd better speed things up. What to wear for tonight's dinner with Sergio? She hadn't given it much thought given all that had happened between the time Sergio had walked her back to her hotel and now. She picked through the clothes, wishing she had packed more pastels and prints. But who knew she'd meet a nice man who wanted to take her to dinner? Minutes ticked by. Carol ultimately pieced together what looked as good a fashion statement as she could make: beige leather flat pumps, a caramel-colored sleeveless sheath belted at the waist with a beige self-tie sash. For jewelry, a simple strand of small clear glass beads and small, silver hoop earrings would do, she decided. She gave herself a head-to-toes assessment before the mirror and liked what she saw. Her look was understated, not at all provocative, maybe even a little boring by some standards. But that's what she wanted. She gave herself another once-over. Something was missing. Carol applied a soft pink coral shade lipstick. There! That was it! *Have lipstick, will travel*. She laughed out loud. She'd have fun tonight; she'd forget about how her family had taken off like three sheets to the wind.

The hotel lobby was crowded. Carol wove through the maze of people checking in, checking out, arriving for dinner, waiting for elevators, summoning porters. For a Friday evening in August, this was not unusual. Venice was awash with tourists during the summer months, especially on the weekends. Sergio was already waiting for her as she made her way through the lobby to the hotel entrance that led to the Floating Patio restaurant.

He had arrived a good half hour early and had ordered himself a glass of Chianti to take the edge off his mood. He was anxious that perhaps Carol would not appreciate a change of venue. He'd arranged a surprise, reservations at Cera's on Giudecca, the classiest restaurant in Venice. Sergio beamed when he saw Carol enter the restaurant. He stood up and caught her attention as she panned the tables.

"Buona sera! Good evening!" Sergio greeted Carol as she approached. He moved quickly to pull out her chair. "Please, sit down, is this comfortable? Can I order you something from the bar?"

Carol stiffened. Sergio had not greeted her Italian style, with a kiss on each cheek. Not that she'd expected it. *Who are you kidding?* she asked herself. *Of course you expected it!*

"Some white wine, please." Carol replied, settling into her chair. *I feel like I'm sitting at your café, Sergio,* she thought. She didn't know what to do with her hands. If only there was a menu she could hold. She placed her hands on her lap.

"How lovely you look this evening," Sergio said. He extended his hand across the table.

I guess he wants to shake hands, Carol thought. She brought one hand up from her lap. Sergio clasped her hand, leaning forward. Instead of a handshake, Sergio gently kissed the top of her hand.

Instinctively, Carol's fingers curled tighter around Sergio's. *Oh my.*

"I am so glad you decided to join me," Sergio said, his voice lower, almost a whisper, as if he wanted to keep this time together their little secret. Carol found it charming. She smiled. This was more like it. For a moment there, she'd worried that the evening would be a dud, in contrast to their enjoyable afternoon the day before yesterday.

Sergio ordered Carol's wine. When it arrived, they saluted the lovely sunset. He watched Carol bring the glass to her lips. *Such beautiful lips*, he thought. She offered him a smile as she lowered her glass. "The wine is delicious," she said.

Sergio returned her smile. *And so are you, Carol Duncan.*

Carol was getting hungry. She'd skipped a mid-day meal to get her hair and nails done.

"Shall we order?" Carol asked Sergio. She hoped Sergio would take the initiative and call for menus. If he didn't she would!

"Yes, of course," Sergio answered. He leaned forward, adding, "The view from Cera's on the Giudecca Canal is so beautiful, Carol." He searched her face for any hint that she recognized the famous restaurant's name.

"I love Giudecca's neighborhoods," Carol volunteered. "I've been to that part of Venice, though not on this trip. You're right, the views from Giudecca Canal are gorgeous." Carol leaned back in her chair. *Could they order now?*

His hint about Cera's seemed to go unnoticed by Carol. Sergio called for a waiter.

Carol grinned. *Thank you!*

The waiter approached. "Check, please," said Sergio.

"The check?" Carol asked. "Aren't we eating?"

Sergio turned to her, his brown eyes sparkling. "We are! But not here. I thought I would surprise you. I made us dinner reservations at Cera's."

It hit her then. She replayed Sergio's brief comment about Giudecca. So, that's why he was dressed to the nines! She'd thought his gray silk suit and burgundy bow tie too formal looking. The Floating Patio was a very nice restaurant, but blazer or sport jacket with an open collar shirt would have worked much better, she thought, especially for early evening dining. Her own wardrobe choice, she'd noticed, had turned out to be perfectly appropriate after all. Most of the women were wearing dresses like hers, summer knits styled with simple lines in neutral shades.

Carol bristled. She knew about Cera's. She also knew that, in a place like that, one did not dress casually, no matter how chic the look. At Cera's, the diamonds came out, so did the haute couture. The women who frequented

Cera's never went to hairdressers, the hairdressers *came to them*.

Shifting her feet from beneath the table, Carol stole a glance at her flat pumps. Her shoes wouldn't do at Cera's any more than would her dress and jewelry. She stood up. "I'm sorry, Sergio," she said. "I can't go. It's—it's out of the way."

Sergio tried to make sense of her words. "Sorry for what? I don't understand. How is Giudecca out of the way? We take the vaporetto and we are there in fifteen minutes."

Carol lowered her eyes. "What I mean is that I'm not dressed for Cera's. I didn't pack anything fancy enough on this trip. I don't even have a pair of high heels with me. And I, I—" Carol stammered. "This is awful, Sergio. I messed up."

Sergio bolted from his chair. "Your dress is perfect, Carol! And do you really think you need high heels?" He moved around the table and placed himself beside her, arm to arm, shoulder to shoulder. Their scant difference in height nonetheless put Carol taller. Sergio turned to her.

"You wear heels, do you know what happens to me? I

end up looking like that science fiction guy from the movies, the incredible shrinking man!" He laughed at his joke, then turned serious. "I would not care if you were twice as tall as me, Carol," he said. "Nobody looks at a person's footwear at Cera's. Nobody cares."

Carol thought, *Of course they don't look at footwear. They can't. The shoes are beneath full-length gowns.*

She looked down at her shoes again and shrugged. Maybe Sergio was right about nobody caring. But the rest of her outfit had to go. Finally she spoke. "Let's just stay here for dinner, Sergio." Carol dropped back into her chair. The evening had barely begun and already she felt exhausted. She would have been better off just ordering room service and turning in early.

As quickly as she sat down, she stood up again. On second thought, she told Sergio, she wasn't even hungry anymore. She kept her demeanor calm, her expression non-threatening, hoping her act belied her deep disappointment at how her evening had soured. But there was nothing she could do. She could never step foot inside Cera's tonight.

"Nonsense, you are famished," Sergio countered. "I can tell. I run a café, and I know a hungry face when I see one." The waiter returned with the check for their wine, and Sergio quickly made good on the bill, passing more than enough Euros to the waiter. "Keep the change," he said. He took Carol's elbow. "Let's go." Sergio said, and proceeded to usher himself and Carol out of the Floating Patio.

They were going to Cera's, plain and simple, and nobody would care if Carol wore sackcloth and ashes. She was exquisite, he told her. Her heart was racing as she followed his lead. Either Sergio Bari was truly smitten by her, though Carol couldn't figure what possibly could have led him there, or, she reasoned, Cera's dining room probably had low lighting and Sergio knew it.

Sergio knew one thing, that Carol didn't suspect. He would spend this evening seeing to it that her Venetian bucket list came true. As soon as they finished dinner at Cera's.

Their waiter had counted his tip and realized how large it was for just wine. Sergio didn't even know what he'd left, and he didn't care. He was a man in a hurry. So was the waiter, who rushed to Sergio, bowing deeply and offering his hand to Sergio.

"Grazie, Signore, thank you! Enjoy your evening!"

Sergio shook hands with the waiter. It was the right thing to do. As a café owner, he knew the importance of good customer relations from both sides of the hospitality business. As he turned to Carol, taking her elbow again, two other waiters, both carrying a large tray of drinks, pulled up on Carol's blind side. Carol swerved to avoid them, dislodging herself from Sergio's grasp.

Seconds later, an earsplitting crash of glassware meeting floor, and ribbons of scotch, bourbon, red and white vino, undulated through the air like kite tails. Napkins and stirrers flew in all directions. Shards of broken glassware lodged between the patio floor planks.

Some of the diners watched the unfortunate accident unfolding around them in shocked silence, others crouched beneath their tables to avoid the flying debris.

Sergio reached out to Carol, taking her hand and pulling her toward him, then easing her in front of him. "I'm right behind you!" he yelled above the chaotic aftermath behind him. He leaned against Carol, protecting her back from the flying debris. Carol felt his hands on her shoulders, urging her to keep moving.

Her ER nursing instincts took over. Pivoting from

Sergio's protective shield she spun around and ran back to the tables. She was sure there were people who needed help. Half of the patio was in shambles. The waiters' collision had a domino effect; after the trays of drinks went flying, so did the waiters. Carol noticed their waiter, who had not been carrying drinks, but who had simply ended up being in the wrong place at the wrong time. He was stooped over on the floor, wincing in pain, a shard of glass sticking out of the top of his hand.

Carol gathered some of the napkins that had fallen from the trays. She approached the waiter and lowered herself to the floor, next to him. He looked at his hand, then at her. "I'm all right," he said. "I can take this glass out of my hand myself."

Carol frowned. "No, let me. I'm a nurse." Before the waiter could argue, she took his hand in hers and carefully removed the shard, then applied pressure to the wound with the napkins. "You may need stitches," Carol told the waiter. "You should go to the hospital. We can take you."

She pointed to Sergio, who had himself backtracked to the tables when he'd figured there was no sense rushing to Cera's after all. His suit was ruined. The mixed drinks and vino had splashed across the back of his jacket, and a leg of his pants was ripped where its cuff caught the sharp edge of an overturned dessert cart, another casualty of the domino effect. A smear of crème brûlée had found its way from the dessert cart to the vamps of his shoes.

The waiter turned toward where Carol was pointing. "Your companion needs more help than I do, Signorina. I am fine, truly," the waiter told Carol. He got up from the floor and in seconds was back in the thick of the chaos, helping his colleagues clean up the mess, one hand still holding pressure to his wound as he uprighted overturned chairs.

Before Carol could protest, Sergio appeared and took her hand. "You helped him," he acknowledged as he led her out of the Floating Patio and through the hotel lobby to the street exit, "but he doesn't need us in the way now. Let's go."

***

If last evening had turned into a disaster, by the looks of the rising waterline on the fondamenta visible from her hotel window, this morning was a total loss. Carol closed the drapes and debated whether to go back to bed or return Elaine's call. Her sister had left a voice message last night while she and Sergio were assessing their own damages after the chaos at the Floating Patio. Fortunately, neither had emerged worse for wear, suffering no injuries from shattered glass and debris, though Sergio's stylish silk suit was a hot mess. Despite the disappointment, they'd managed to share a chuckle. Here Carol had worried that her ensemble wasn't appropriate for dinner at Cera's, but it was Sergio who ended up having to go home to change his clothes! They decided to call it an evening, and agreed to try it again tonight, if she had time. She had all the time in the world, she told him. As he escorted her to her hotel Carol explained how her brother and sister had taken off, each with their own agenda that didn't include her.

"Then we both have time," Sergio assured her as he walked her to the hotel elevator. "I, too, have nothing pressing for tomorrow. Same time, different place?" he asked with a wink.

Carol suggested she meet him at his own café. She loved Caffe La Rosa, and wanted to spend more time enjoying the vibes along the Via Garibaldi before her vacation was over. And besides, she added, she thought Caffe La Rosa's cappuccino was tops.

Sergio kissed her hand. "Tomorrow evening at six, then. I will be waiting at my café, with cappuccino!"

This morning's rain was falling hard and fast. Carol finally remembered Elaine's call when she reached for her phone to pull up the local weather forecast. Carol scolded herself. *Dummy! How can you forget to call back your own sister?*

Scenes of last evening surfaced like the high waters of Venice in a rainstorm, hard, fast, unrelenting: the Floating Patio, before the chaos, her hand receiving his kiss, outside her room, in the quiet corridor, *tomorrow at six*, another kiss upon her hand, his suit ruined. He still looked like a million. He'd left her feeling like royalty in her plain beige dress.

Sergio Bari. That's how.

Chapter 12

Sipping his morning espresso, Sergio stood at his kitchen window and watched the rain as it descended in sheets into the narrow canal. The contractors surely would not be working inside his Libreria Acqua Alta today. He hoped the work completed thus far would hold. It had been weeks since he had had to close the popular bookstore for much-needed repairs. Too bad things had not turned out so well the night before, he reflected. He'd had it all planned to take Carol to the Libreria after dinner and give her a private tour of its interior. It would not look like the photographs Carol had seen in magazines, not with all the construction going on, and the famous bathtub temporarily removed. But a visit to the Libreria Acqua Alta was on Carol's wish list, and he was determined to make her wish come true.

The thud of a door knocker hitting against the thick oak door below his second floor apartment interrupted his quiet reflection. Sergio wondered who would venture outside on such a morning. He drew closer to the window, his nose almost hitting the glass, and peered down to the narrow pavement which by then was puddled with the overflow of rainwater from the canal.

It was Paolo. A very nervous-looking Paolo, Sergio observed. His friend was pacing back and forth like a nervous father-to-be. Had Anna delivered? No, it was too early. But something was up, and Sergio grabbed his umbrella and rushed barefoot out of his apartment, taking the building's old stone steps two at a time to ground level. He opened the door and extended his umbrella to his friend. "Paolo! Take this! What are you doing out? Is Anna all right?"

Paolo ignored Sergio's questions. He took the umbrella, opened it, then looked down at Sergio's bare feet. "Leonora Santella came back!" he blurted. "Put your boots on, man! She's waiting for you!"

His friend's words hit Sergio like a lightning bolt. He reeled backward, almost losing his balance. "Where? Where is she?" he croaked.

"I don't know now. She was at Bibi's last night. I was there. I saw her for the first time. She was talking to the bartender. He made her a drink, she asked him a lot of questions. I just sat and listened, played dumb. She was looking for *you*, she said. She called you her *first love*." Paolo took a breath. "I wanted to call you last night, but it was late. So I came right over first thing." The rain was falling harder. The umbrella was no longer useful under the sheer weight of the downpour. A rogue squall funneled through the narrow street, splashing over Paolo's galoshes to his calves.

Paolo closed the umbrella and tossed it back to Sergio. Pulling his rain parka hood over his head, he turned to go. "I have to get back. Anna's parents are supposed to go home today but with this weather, who knows? I will keep an eye on Bibi's. If I see her go in, I will stall her. But I won't tell her I know you."

Sergio heard Paolo's words, but his friend's account made no sense at all. Leonora Santella, back here, in Venice? Looking for him, at Bibi's? Why Bibi's? Leonora had always known the location Caffe La Rosa. It was his family's business, established in the same spot on the Via Garibaldi as it stood today. She had been there often when they were going together. Didn't she remember?

Leonora could not have known to look for him at Bibi's. She would not have known Paolo and Anna Trezzi were his friends, and had not even lived in Venice when she was still living here.

I will stall her, Sergio now recalled Paolo saying before racing back to Bibi's. Sergio sat on the bottom step in the vestibule stairwell. Carol's image flashed before him as he remembered her the day he had helped her on the stairs of the shop on the Via Garibaldi. He needed to steady himself. Both his head and heart were on overdrive, creating a tug of war between reason and instinct. The weight of having to make a decision pressed against his chest harder than the heavy rains falling from the sky. After a minute, he got up and climbed the stairs back to his apartment to call Bibi's. Rocco, the bartender, answered on the first ring.

Sergio got right to the point. "Rocco. Sergio Bari. A woman was at your bar last night looking for me. Tell me what you know."

"Yes, Sergio. A woman named Leonora Santella. Looking for you," Rocco answered.

Sergio heard a muffled exchange at the other end.

"Sergio?" A different voice. Paolo's.

"Paolo? Where's Rocco?"

"Right here. Are you coming?"

Sergio took a deep breath. "No, I am not." He had no idea when he'd made that decision, but there it was. His heartbeat slowed, and he felt better. It was done. *He* was done. Done with the decade long obsession with a girl he used to know, a girl he thought he loved, who had now returned. Could the timing be worse? He'd met the lovely American, Carol Duncan, and for days he'd convinced himself she was Leonora's twin, all because the two shared a look. But deeper than looks, Sergio realized the more he and Carol talked and walked together and shared their stories, Leonora and Carol were no more alike than he and Paolo, even though both he and his friend sported dark wavy hair, brown eyes and were of a shorter stature than either would have chosen, if given an option. But the similarities stopped there.

It dawned on Sergio that his obsessive need to connect Carol and Leonora had driven him to snoop around the Libreria Acqua Alta not once but twice, following Carol before he'd even met her, observing her ponder the *Closed* sign on the door, noticing how she tensed, then turned around and walked quickly away. He'd thought about what he could have done instead, had asked himself a dozen times since why he hadn't simply approached her, introduced himself, and explained that the Libreria was temporarily closed for repairs? *Stupido!* He would not behave stupidly anymore. There would be no more comparing the lovely, sweet American lady with Leonora Santella. By not seeing Leonora, Sergio reasoned, he would not be tempted to fall back into his obsession. He would not be reckless, silly, stupid or worried when it came to Leonora Santella. He would not go to her.

Rocco came back to the phone. "Sergio? What do I tell this Santella woman when she comes to my bar again? She said she would be back."

Sergio looked out the window. The rain was subsiding. Good. Maybe Cosimo would be able to set up the outdoor seating today after all.

"Send her to Caffe La Rosa," he replied, again his words seemingly taking on a life of their own. "If she asks for the address, give it to her. If she does not ask, don't offer it." He shut off his phone, and poured himself another espresso. Yes. Leonora Santella could come to him. It made perfect sense. After all, hadn't she been the one to leave in the first place?

Chapter 13

Carol read Elaine's brief text: *We're home, everything great, more soon! XOXO E&A.*

A wave of relief fell over her. She'd waited for what seemed an eternity to hear from her sister. Even these few words were better than nothing. Carol shut off her phone. No interruptions allowed this evening, starting now. The last thing Carol wanted was anything further getting in the way of her and Sergio's second try at an evening out, even if their meeting place this time was his café rather than her hotel. They'd agreed not to be seen at the Floating Patio again, at least not together!

Carol loved the Via Garibaldi and didn't mind taking a walk there this evening to share some vino and dolce with Sergio, but there was more she wanted to do and see. It was disappointing enough she'd not yet realized her wish to visit the Libreria Acqua Alta, let alone taking a midnight gondola ride. Besides, who would accompany her? Couples deeply in love took midnight gondola rides, not ER nurses with a history of false starts when it came to romance.

Dinner with Sergio Bari would have to do, and, Carol

had to admit, she enjoyed his company more than she'd anticipated, even when all hell broke loose! *He seems to enjoy my company, too*, she thought as she dipped her toes into the warm bathwater. She adjusted the water massage settings and lowered herself into the tub. The pulsing water massage felt so good, she could stay in this tub all evening. It would be even nicer if Sergio joined her, right here in her room, just the two of them, maybe with some wine and candles to set the mood. And bubbles! That would be the icing on the cake! She let her mind wander and closed her eyes, enjoying the warmth of her bath, imagining Sergio was with her. How long had it been since she'd fantasized like this, not to mention the sensations that built with those fantasies. Her body throbbed with anticipation of what might happen later that evening with Sergio Bari. As quickly as she allowed her fantasies to take her away, she forced herself not to get to a point of no return. She and Sergio would not be ending up in her bathtub tonight. He was too much a gentleman to make a move like that so soon. And she'd never take the initiative. Carol felt her face flush at the very idea of luring Sergio to any bathtubs, unless it was the one at the Libreria Acqua Alta, of course! But that wasn't happening, either.

She rubbed the back of her neck with the soothing natural fiber sponge, thinking of questions she wanted to ask Sergio when she saw him later. *Where do you live? What is your place like? Do you have a balcony? Is it far from your café?* Would Sergio think her questions too probing, as if she wanted to know where he went when he wasn't with her or at work? She felt her face flush, and not from the warmth of the bathwater. She really did want to know these things, and more. Slipping into another fantasy, Carol gave up trying to justify her curiosity. She closed her eyes again. Do you sleep in a single bed or a double bed, Sergio? Do you prefer a quick shower or a long, leisurely soak? Who washes your back? Would you wash mine if you were here? She filled her bath sponge again and squeezed the water over her shoulders, imaging Sergio behind her, lathering her skin, massaging her back in a way no pulsating water jets ever could. A small moan escaped her throat. She felt her body sink again, deeper into the water, imagining the warmth was emanating from Sergio Bari's embrace, gently enveloping her, holding her close, seducing her just like Giacomo Casanova seduced the convent nuns.

It was all she could do to force herself to get out of the tub. If she didn't keep her head on straight, she'd drown. Maybe not in the tub, maybe not in the *acqua alta* of Venice in a downpour, but drown she would, for sure. She'd drown in thoughts and feelings for Sergio Bari. Even alone in her room, Carol felt Sergio all over her. It scared her. *He* scared her, so much so that, to her astonishment, Carol realized how much she missed the edgy excitement that came with taking a risk. The excitement of feeling scared.

She combed her hair, thinking, *I'm going back to the Libreria before I leave this city, no matter if I sense somebody watching me, or if I hear strange sounds. It's probably just the old streets and houses groaning under the weight of time and water.* Even if the Libreria was still closed, it was no time to be timid. How much longer would she be here, five days, six? The first week had flown by because Randy and Elaine were with her, the weather had been great for walking, and the three of them had enjoyed themselves, each in their own ways, but still sticking together. Elaine's husband was a darling, but the moment Al arrived, Carol had sensed that Elaine would opt out of their "just us gals" adventure in favor of spending time with him. But she hadn't anticipated her sister actually flying back home a scant week into their vacation! Through all the rapid change of plans, when Elaine finally reached out to her on WhatsApp, Carol felt the shifting sands of circumstance settle down. With her sister back on hometown soil, and Randy traipsing around Venice with Vicky Potts, Carol was on her own time now. She could use it or lose it.

Wrapped in her robe, Carol moved to the bedroom, turned her phone on again, then set about choosing her clothes for the evening. Something to wow Sergio would be nice. Then she remembered how uncomfortable she'd felt at the Floating Patio when Sergio had divulged his plans to take her to dinner at the ultra upscale Cera's. She thought she wasn't dressed for Cera's, but Sergio hadn't cared what she was wearing. He just wanted her by his side.

An incoming text alert interrupted the quiet of her room. Carol picked up her phone. It was another WhatsApp message from Elaine: *Nxt Yr JUST U&ME!*

I understand! Glad you two lovebirds are home safe! Carol responded before moving a voice mail from Randy that had come in while her phone was turned off. There was loud music in the background. Carol couldn't make out all of Randy's message details but let it go. At least he'd remembered to check in. She sent a quick text: *Have fun, Ciao, you two!*

Carol heard a sound coming from the connecting room. It couldn't be Randy and Vicky. Carol knocked on the connecting door. "Anybody home?" she called. No answer. She tried the doorknob. It was locked. She knocked again, and this time, the door unlocked. A bone-thin, older woman opened the door. She wore blue rubber gloves and a light blue smock with the hotel logo embroidered on the front. Her name tag introduced her as Pia. Her thin lips were pursed below an even thinner nose.

Pia frowned as she took a step back and looked Carol up and down. "Can I help you." Her question was a statement.

"I... I'm sorry," Carol stammered, noticing the woman's name tag. She tried again. "Forgive me for interrupting, Pia. I'm looking for Randy, I mean, *Randall* Duncan. I'm his sister. We booked these connecting rooms."

Pia stepped to the side and pulled a clipboard from the

basket of cleaning supplies set beside a waiting vacuum sweeper.

Carol resisted the urge to cross the now unobstructed threshold. It was, after all, Randy's room, not hers, even though he wasn't occupying it much lately. She wanted to snoop around, but Pia's all-business expression was a giveaway that Carol had interrupted the woman from her work and she was in no mood to linger for small talk let alone look for missing guests.

Pia returned to her side of the threshold, closing any last-minute opportunity Carol had of making a visual sweep of Randy's room. Her boney fingers ran down the list attached to the clipboard. She shook her head with each name she read aloud. Finally, she jabbed at the guest list and thrust the clipboard at Carol.

"*Vede. See.* No Duncan but one. Carol. *You* are Carol Duncan."

Carol nodded. "Yes, I am." She started to read the names of the guests to herself. There was no mistake, no computer printout error. Randy's name was nowhere on the guest list.

"Grazie, Pia," Carol said, handing Pia the clipboard. She reached for the doorknob, but Pia beat her to it, and slammed the door shut.

Carol bit her lip. If Randy checked out of the hotel, he'd have no place to go if Vicky decided to cut him loose. He'd return to Carol and ask if he could crash in the extra bed left vacant in her and Elaine's room when Elaine relocated to the Honeymoon Suite with Albert. *No way*, she muttered. It was enough that her brother had landed on her couch back home after the Joyce catastrophe. She wasn't about to put him up again. She opened her phone and replayed Randy's voice message, concentrating with extra effort. After three attempts, she was able to catch the entire message despite the music in the mix: *Sis, I'm with Vicky until we leave for our trip but right now we're at a club on Lido Beach so I hope you get this. We'll catch up with you. Cheeow!* Carol cringed. What trip? The one they would take back home in a week? A different trip? What was he talking about? She was even more confused now. Randy never mentioned any intention of checking out of their hotel. But it looked like he had done just that. None of this made sense. And here she'd thought she was merely distracted when Randy's message didn't make sense to her the *first* time she'd listened to it. What was that brother of hers up to?

Why had he burned his bridges this way? There must be a mistake. There had to be.

Carol called the front desk. The concierge confirmed that Randall Duncan had checked out of the connecting room.

"He did leave a message for Carol Duncan," the concierge added. "You are Signorina Duncan?"

"Yes, don't you remember me?" Carol replied. She felt her patience waning fast. What was it with the hotel staff today? *First the room attendant gives me the Evil Eye and now the concierge needs proof that I'm me!* She sighed into the receiver. "What's the message, please?"

"It is here," replied the concierge. "Shall we deliver it to your room, Signorina?"

Carol rolled her eyes. *I said what, not where.* "No," she answered. "I'll be down in ten minutes to pick it up myself, *grazie*." She smirked at the receiver before slamming it into its cradle. *I'm turning into Pia*, she thought briefly, before another revelation pushed away all thoughts of the unfriendly room attendant. *Sergio Bari.* The last time a message was left for her at the hotel's front desk, it had been from Sergio, inviting her to dinner. How many days ago was that? She couldn't remember.

When she was with Sergio, time seemed not to matter.

Were they still on for tonight? Carol looked out the window. The morning's rain storm had long passed. No call had come in from Sergio to cancel plans due to *acqua alta*. She returned to her closet, ultimately settling on a sleek two-piece black and white ensemble. She added a necklace, a single strand of silver chain. Nice enough. Then she put on the heels she'd purchased on a lark earlier today. She'd stand noticeably taller than Sergio in these shoes, she knew. But Carol sensed Sergio wouldn't mind at all. He had made it clear at the Floating Patio that he wanted to spend time with her no matter what kind of shoes she wore.

Carol glanced at the wide-brimmed sun visor Albert had purchased for her. She'd worn it the first time she and Sergio actually talked, the day he helped her down the flight of stairs when she'd had a fit of coughing. Should she wear it to the lobby to retrieve her brother's message? Its enormous brim would surely hide any disappointment her eyes might reveal if she received any more unexpected news!

Whatever Randy's note had to say, whether it was an apology, or a request for money, or an engagement announcement for that matter, nothing he and Vicky were up to would get in the way of this evening with Sergio. Not if she could help it.

Chapter 14

She could not be Leonora. Impossible. Not in a million years could the woman standing before him, greeting him so aggressively, be the, sweet, soft-spoken young lady he'd fallen in love with over a decade ago. Sergio wanted to recoil from her arms, arms that gripped him in a bear hug and swayed him from left to right. Loud humming escaped her throat and filled his mouth as she kissed him long and hard.

Sergio managed to free himself long enough to catch a breath before Leonora had him in her grip again. This time, her hands clutched the shoulders of his suit jacket. She looked at him and whistled. "Look at you! And you dressed up just for me! How ARE ya, my Babba Loop?"

Babba Loop? Where did *that* come from? Sergio didn't want to know. Leonora told him anyway.

"You don't mind if I call you my Babba Loop, do ya? It's my pied butcherbird's name. He has a great croon. You still croon, Sergiii? Remember when you use to croon love songs to me?"

What is a pied butcherbird? he wondered. He made a mental note to google it later.

"You have the wrong guy," Sergio answered. "I'm a lousy crooner." He couldn't hold his own in a Karaoke competition, let alone romance a woman with his singing voice.

He led Leonora to the interior of his café. As he poured some wine for them, he couldn't help berating himself for even thinking of entertaining her. Hadn't he wasted enough time all these years hoping Leonora would return? And now, here she was. *Back in town, visiting old haunts*, as she described her impromptu visit.

"I'm married, you know," Leonora stated matter-of-factly as she took her seat. She guzzled her drink like a sailor on shore leave. "I'm Leonora Santella-Sellersby now." Leonora spoke of her new life, of her marriage to an insurance agent, their home in the woods of North Carolina, of their two boys—she showed him the kids' photos, but the husband remained anonymous. Her mother lived with them now. Leonora had convinced Signora Santella to move to the States so that she could have "quality time" with her grandsons. Her mother fell for it, Leonora told Sergio, a conspiratorial gleam in her eyes.

"We really needed a full-time babysitter. My husband

and I like to travel."

"Your husband is here with you?" Sergio asked. He had found Leonora waiting alone outside his café, but did that mean she was in Venice without him? Sergio didn't want to pry, but Leonora answered his question, and a lot more.

"We travel separately. We sleep in separate beds these days, too. But our marriage is solid. We're on the same page even if we're not under the same covers, if you know what I mean."

No, Leonora. I have no idea what you mean, Sergio wanted to tell her. Instead he smiled and refilled her glass. "Yes, of course," he said diplomatically. He wished she would leave. *So why did I delay her with more vino?* he asked himself, just as quickly shaking off the question. This glass, too, Leonora emptied in record time.

She was thirty-one years old now, she volunteered. And still attractive, Sergio thought. But looks weren't everything to him anymore. He'd grown up. There had to be more than a pretty face to keep his interest. Even during his man-about-town phase, dating this blonde and that brunette, the red heads, the bald heads, the spiked and pierced heads, whatever the fashion statement of the moment, Sergio, nevertheless, had avoided getting serious with any of the women he dated. They were all lovely in their own way, but something was missing. He'd visited the home of one of his dates in a rare acceptance of a dinner invitation out of the public eye. He'd noticed her home lacked books, yet dozens of high fashion magazines littered the coffee table, and the bathroom overflowed with more cosmetics and perfumes than someone would need in a lifetime, in his opinion. Why the preoccupation with looks? But hadn't he done the same thing? Had he not become Mister Meticulous, even garnering a cover shot in one of the regional menswear trade magazines?

Sergio told Leonora she looked wonderful. His compliment earned him another risk of getting caught in a bear hug.

"You toooo, my gorgeous Babba Loop!" Leonora giggled as she reached across the table, arms extended, winding around Sergio's neck. Sergio gently released Leonora's hands from his jacket collar. Leonora sat back in her chair and giggled like a little kid who had just stumped a grownup with a riddle. She was obviously buzzed.

Sergio giggled, too, not knowing what else to do. What he did know from listening to Leonora's rapid fire recount of her life after Venice, after him, was indisputable: she was not the Leonora Santella he had loved, or thought he had loved, when she was nineteen and in a hurry to take on the world. All similarity stopped with her looks. Everything else had changed, even her name. She was Leonora Santella-Sellersby now. After only three years with the airlines, she chucked it all in for a picket fence and front porch life in rural North Carolina.

Leonora pulled a cigarette from her purse.

"Do you mind?" she asked Sergio, holding the unlit cigarette out to him.

Sergio reached behind him to a small stand. Two bowls sat on the stand. One offered tiny pillow-shaped after-dinner mints. The second bowl offered matchbooks, each embellished with a yellow rose, Caffe La Rosa's logo, on the front flap.

Sergio lifted both bowls from the stand and placed them on their table.

"Freebies for our patrons. Help yourself," he said, forcing smile. He wasn't big on mints, and he hated cigarettes. But, the customer's wishes had to come first and, for all intents and purposes, Leonora Sellersby was a customer, albeit not a paying one. The vino he poured for her was on the house. Leonora had to realize this, given she gladly accepted a third glass to go with her Merit Lights.

He lit her cigarette for her. *The Leonora I knew never smoked*, he thought. *Am I being too critical or is she smoking in front of me now because she remembers that I do not use tobacco?* Self-analysis wasn't one of Sergio's strong suits. He beat himself up too much playing that game. But the questions kept poking at him, silly, petty worrisome questions that he knew he shouldn't waste his time trying to answer.

Why am I lighting her cigarettes after placing an entire bowl of matchbooks in front of her? Why the mints? Do I want her to think she has bad breath from the wine and tobacco? Am I expecting her to give me another kiss? Sergio felt trapped. *Mamma Mia! If only she would leave!*

He rose briefly to hunt down an ashtray. *Watch her drop it*, he thought, as memories of last night at the Floating Patio surfaced out of nowhere. He handed the ashtray to Leonora. Her hand slightly trembled as she took it from him. Yep, she was soused. *No more vino for you, Signora Sellersby*, Sergio decided. He poured what little remained in the bottle into his own glass. If Leonora expected more refreshment, she'd have to find her way back to Bibi's. Sergio was expecting Carol to show within the hour. The sooner Leonora finished her story the better.

"Please, go on," Sergio said.

Leonora knotted her brow. "Say what?"

Sergio winced. *Say what?* The Leonora he remembered never talked slang. He waved his hand as if trying to shoo her question away.

"Your story," he prompted. "You were telling me about what happened in your life since leaving Venice."

"Ah, yes, my story," she said, taking a drag of her cigarette. She exhaled slowly, speaking through the smoke. "The airport. That's where my husband and I met. I don't remember which airport. O'Hare, JFK, LAX, they all look alike after a while, you know. Anyway, it was love, or maybe lust, at first sight. I never fell that hard for anyone before. I can't live without him."

Sergio frowned. Leonora wasn't making any sense.

Did three glasses of vino really tune her out or was she just playing with him?

"But you said you and your husband travel separately, and you seem to be doing just fine without him right now," Sergio ventured, surprising himself for cross examining her like that. Leonora didn't seem to mind.

"Yes, I'm fine right now. And how are you? You haven't told me what you've been up to all these years."

"I was *up to* longing for you and me to get back together. While I waited, I dated a lot. And of course, I took over the café. Do you remember this place?"

Leonora's eyes swept the café interior. "Maybe. Yes. Of course. But we sat outside, I almost forgot. You and me. Your parents set something up for us once."

"Your birthday," Sergio recalled. "I didn't have to bus the tables that evening. My parents gave me time off to celebrate your birthday. We had a cake. I gave you a necklace. Do you still have it?"

"You gave me a necklace, Babba Loop?" Leonora asked.

"Costume jewelry. I was on a bare-bones salary at the time," Sergio replied, grinning. "It was a long time ago."

"Must have been, Babba Loop! I'm drawing a blank!"

You're buzzed. Sergio thought, rising from his seat. It was time he sent her on her way, but first, maybe, some espresso would help her sober up.

"I will get you some coffee," he offered.

"No, Babba Loop, no coffee, I have to go. Just wanted to find you."

It was now or never. If he didn't ask her why she wanted to find him, he'd never know if she still cared for him, even a little.

"Leonora, I—" he started, but Leonora cut him off. She stood, swayed just enough to confirm what Sergio suspected, that she'd drunk too much vino. A twinge of guilt surfaced. Had he plied her with alcohol to get her to talk? No, his better angel told him.

"Can I call you a private water taxi?" he asked her.

"No, Babba Loop. Just tell me you love me."

Had he heard right? Before he could answer, Leonora was out the door, weaving her way through the outdoor seating Cosimo was preparing. He had come in early to wipe the outdoor tables and chairs dry from the earlier rains. Sergio called out to his waiter. "Cosimo! Detain the lady for a moment, please!"

Cosimo ran interference as Sergio reached into one of

the cut-flower buckets that graced the entrance to the café. He pulled a yellow rose from the arrangement and hurried toward the street before Leonora could dodge Cosimo.

"Leonora!" Sergio called out. "I have another gift for you!"

Cosimo stepped aside once Sergio was face to face with Leonora.

"Good work." Sergio winked to his waiter. Sergio extended the long-stemmed rose to Leonora. "For you."

Leonora snatched the rose from Sergio's hand and placed its stem between her teeth. Without so much as a parting glance, she turned away, swaying onto the Via Garibaldi like a boat bobbing in a breeze.

Cosimo shrugged and returned to his duties. Sergio stood in stunned silence, his mind racing. *I gave Leonora a rose, but I didn't tell her I love her. What was the rose supposed to do, speak for me?*

It wasn't until he saw Carol Duncan walking toward the café that Sergio realized he'd given Leonora the rose not as an expression of love and affection, but simply to say goodbye.

Chapter 15

"Have you decided where we'll have dinner?" Sergio asked Carol. He pulled out a chair for her. "Or was that my job?" he added jokingly.

Carol grinned. "Well, we know we're not going to Cera's." She reached across the table, patting his hand. "Wherever you want to go is fine with me, Sergio. I think I'm dressed for it."

Sergio appraised her look. "You should be on the cover of *Italian Vogue*."

"No way." Carol felt a flush building beneath the collar of her blouse.

"Vero! It is true!" Sergio replied. "You are a, come si dice? A *babe*!" A compliment like that would get him canceled by every woman on Match.com, Carol thought, suppressing a laugh. In truth, she loved that Sergio called her a babe, and she didn't mind letting him know it.

"Grazie, Sergio, that's the nicest thing anybody has said to me all day." Carol had hoped Sergio would like her black palazzo pants and white silk blouse. Several gentlemen who passed her on her way to Caffe La Rosa had noticed her, and their appreciative glances were hard to ignore.

"I'm sorry about last evening, how everything went so badly," Sergio offered.

"Don't be. It was nothing compared to what I found out earlier today," Carol replied. Her warm smile faded before Sergio's eyes, alarming him. Carol caught his concern. She patted his hand again, feeling like the ER nurse she was, always offering assurance and encouragement to her patients that she was there for them. Nobody else seemed to need her. Randy's note hadn't quite sunk in yet. She was now the only Duncan sibling in town. Her family had taken off, one after the other, and without so much as a day's notice of their intentions.

Sergio was looking at her with deepening concern, she could see that. Would sharing Randy's note ruin their evening? Carol pondered the risk. Could anything have gone more badly than last evening? Yet, here they were, together as planned, trying again to have what Carol came to look at as a date, neatly planned and packaged. Why then, did she feel that her best time since getting to know Sergio Bari had been when they walked and talked over a couple of cones of gelato?

Carol pulled Randy's note from her purse and read it to Sergio. She wasn't prepared for Sergio's reaction any more than she'd anticipated her own when she first read it at the lobby desk. News of where Randy was going with Vicky had stunned her. "Mamma Mia! What an adventure! It is wonderful in the Dolomites. He and the lady will have a great time, especially this time of year! It's a fun road trip. Many of the tourists do it."

Carol waved the note back and forth, as if doing so would erase the words. "This is not good, Sergio. My brother can't go galivanting all over the place, let alone in the *mountains*! He has a job back home, he needs to find a new apartment. What if he doesn't get back?" Carol shuddered.

"He will be back, he and the lady," Sergio interrupted. "He's saying that." Sergio pointed to the note still in Carol's hand. "He's telling you this. 'We will catch up with you.' He says right here in black and white. Why not believe it?"

Carol glanced at the paper again and sighed. "You're right. I'm overreacting. He met Vicky here, and it turns out she lives not far from us back home. Small world, huh?"

Sergio smiled. "Very small. In fact, I met…" He stopped himself. "Never mind. Are you hungry?"

"A little," Carol replied. "Randy's stunt messed up my appetite. I hardly ate anything today." She put Randy's note back in her purse. "Well, I'm not going to cry over spilled milk, as they say. We should keep to our plans."

And I won't, either Sergio thought. He skirted the table and helped Carol out of her chair. As she lifted her soft white pashmina shawl to her shoulders, Sergio gently took it from her hands and wrapped it around her. Who knew when or if he'd see Carol Duncan again after tonight. He could only hope the evening he had in store would keep him in her thoughts, maybe even in her heart, long after she returned to New Jersey. He took her elbow. "Let's go," he whispered, whisking Carol onto the Via Garibaldi before she had a chance to change her mind.

***

From across their table at a small restaurant on Calle Crosera, Carol met Sergio's question with a blank stare. "The lady you said you saw who looked drunk and acted crazy playing with a yellow rose, did she look familiar?

Do you think she looked like you?"

He has to be kidding, Carol thought. "Of course not," she said, trying to be serious. He looked so earnest, but the question was absurd. "I mean, I never saw her before."

"Do you remember what she looked like?" Sergio asked.

"Yes, she was tall and had dark hair," Carol answered.

"She looked like you?" Sergio pressed.

Carol gasped. "Absolutely not! I'm not drunk and I'm not crazy!"

Her stomach suddenly growled loudly enough for Sergio to raise his eyebrows. "Was that you?"

Carol nodded, her cheeks turning crimson in the light of the candle. "I'm sorry, I didn't realize I was so hungry."

Their eyes again locked from across the table. *He's acting weird*, Carol thought.

She must think I'm nuts, Sergio thought. The waiter appeared with their appetizers, breaking the awkwardness that had passed between them. Carol devoured her shrimp cocktail, Sergio dug into each escargot with relish. Anything to avoid talking about the woman with the rose.

Carol didn't doubt that the poor creature was more than buzzed, swinging her rose up and down and side to side as if she was conducting an orchestra with a baton, meandering from the Riva degli Schiavoni to a nearby fondamenta, then back to the Riva as if on an evening stroll to nowhere, all the while grunting *babbaloop babbaloop* between hiccups. That rose, too, made no sense. It looked exactly like those in the cut-flower buckets that were placed at the entrance of the door to the interior seating area at Caffe La Rosa. But there were many cut flowers arranged in similar buckets, all over Venice. *See one yellow rose, see them all*, Carol thought, dismissing the notion that Sergio may have seen the woman before, and maybe had even given her that rose. That Sergio had gone so far as to ask her if the woman she'd described looked like her nagged at Carol. She couldn't let it go.

Sergio spoke up, bringing her back to the present. "How was the shrimp?"

"Delicious," Carol answered. She scanned the cozy room. The restaurant had only a dozen tables, but every one was occupied.

"This must be a popular place, yes?" Carol

volunteered. "It's packed. We were lucky to get in without a reservation."

Sergio grinned. He felt more relaxed now that Carol seemed to welcome changing the subject.

"I know the owner of this restaurant," he admitted. "I'm sure that when he saw us walk in, he took one look at you and knew he had to seat us at the best table."

Whoa, that's way too much, Carol thought, smiling back. A compliment was one thing, but this was going overboard. She decided to try again.

"Do you know her? The lady with the rose? Is she from the neighborhood?"

Uh-oh. Sergio checked his watch. He hoped their meal would arrive soon.

"The lady?" he asked, trying to stall the inevitable.

Carol bristled. "The *drunk* lady by the fondamenta on the Riva. Waving her yellow rose and speaking gibberish. The rose looked like the ones you have outside your café."

Sergio shifted in his chair. Why was he holding back? What difference would it make if he told Carol what had happened earlier today? After all he hadn't made the scene, Leonora had. And he didn't force her to drink so much. Leonora got herself drunk.

"She could have held her hand over the top of the glass when I offered her more vino," he thought out loud.

"What was that?" Carol asked.

"Nothing," Sergio replied. He didn't like himself right now. It wasn't in his nature to justify why he did this or that. He was Italian! Italians live by their passion! Forget all that analytical back and forth! Viva the Italian way, his way! Or was it? He felt cornered, but held his tongue, shrugging off Carol's questions in favor of raving about their main course, which, thankfully, had arrived at their table before Carol could probe further on the topic of "the drunk lady". He was relieved when, after finishing their main course, Carol had opted for a walk over staying for dessert. He'd planned meticulously, down to the private water taxi meeting them at the fondamenta San Lorenzo to whisk them to the Libreria Acqua Alta, and later, to a waiting gondola.

***

Carol stood speechless inside the gutted Libreria Acqua Alta. She still couldn't process all that Sergio had divulged just minutes ago, when they were aboard the private water taxi. It was enough of a surprise when he'd told her that he was taking her this evening. "I thought this bookshop was closed," she told him upon learning their destination.

He'd placed an old-fashioned skeleton key in the palm of her hand, closing her fingers around it with his own, holding onto her hand longer than he needed to, but not nearly for as long as he wanted to, Carol had sensed. His gesture gave her tingling sensations, but not the frightening kind that had surfaced when she came to the bookshop on her own and stood outside, hearing sounds she wasn't sure were real but sensing that someone, somewhere close by, was watching her every move.

"This is my shop." Sergio spoke softly as he stood next to her. "Almost," he added.

Carol finally found her voice. "What do you mean?"

Sergio explained that he was one of several trusted associates of the legal owner, who was presently out of the country. "I offered to serve as a caretaker of this shop while it was undergoing renovations in the owner's absence. We have a gentlemen's agreement that I will buy Libreria Acqua Alta when the owner is ready to part with it."

"How wonderful, Sergio," Carol replied. What more could she say? She'd never want the responsibility of keeping this shop afloat, literally. But it was obvious that Sergio was determined to carry on with overseeing the extensive work being done.

Sergio edged closer to Carol's side and took her elbow, guiding her carefully to another section of the room.

"Actually, I feel like I own this place already," Sergio said as they navigated lengths of wood, tool boxes, hammers, and saws left on the floor, waiting for the next day's work.

She could understand that, Carol told him, "Sometimes I am so wrapped up in my feelings that I believe something is true when it's really just my wish that it were true."

Sergio flinched. She was going to ask about Leonora again. Her comment was her signal, wasn't it? Why would she have elaborated that way if she wasn't fishing for some truth? Surely his question had been beyond ridiculous, and it had given him away. He knew the drunk lady holding the yellow rose. It was time Carol knew her, too. *I have to tell her now*. He released Carol's elbow, turned to face her, fighting the urge to take her in his arms to run his fingers through the soft silk that was her hair. He simply stood there before her, concealed by the shadows cast by the weak lighting in the shop. *All the better*, he thought. *I don't want to see the look you are going to give me, Carol Duncan, after I spill my guts*.

"Carol, I want to—" A rap at the door of the Libreria Acqua Alta interrupted. The gondolier had arrived with the second part of Sergio's surprise for Carol. He let go of Carol's shoulders and again took her elbow. "It's here," he said, walking her around more construction materials, retracing their steps toward the door.

"What's here? Who?" Carol whispered. She drew herself closer to Sergio. She was getting that creepy feeling again. Were they both being followed now? Sergio kept silent. He opened the door, greeted the gondolier and introduced him to Carol.

"Please, seat her aboard while I lock up."

Carol followed the gondolier to the edge of the narrow canal. A beautiful gondola was waiting, bobbing between the red and white striped poles that jutted above the water line. It had not been there when they disembarked from the private water taxi. Another surprise, Carol guessed. Where was he taking her now? She asked the gondolier but he did not understand English. Carol reverted to her second language skills. "Dove andiamo, Signore?"

The gondolier raised a finger and grinned as he made a zipping motion across his lips, then shrugged his shoulders, feigning ignorance. Carol gave him a wry smile in return. *I get it. You have to play dumb.* She settled into the comfortable burgundy-velvet-cushioned loveseat. Moments later, Sergio was by her side again. As the gondolier steered his craft toward the wide expanse of the Grand Canal, Sergio placed his arm around the back of the loveseat and turned her head gently with a brush of his hand beneath her soft chin.

"May I hold you?" he asked timidly.

Carol snuggled closer to him, her gesture answering his question. Whatever was on Sergio's mind, and surely something was on his mind, Carol decided then and there not to kill this special moment with words. She hoped he would keep silent, too, as they moved along the Grand Canal. The view was magnificent, the water shining like black ice, the moon above them so big and bright tonight. A full moon. The timing could not be better. To be riding in a gondola on the Grand Canal with a full moon in the star-filled night sky and someone by her side who, even if only for a little while, wanted to be with her, to show her a lovely evening in this lovely city. Someone who enjoyed her company. But did he want something more? More importantly, did *she*? *If I give him the high sign, there's no looking back.* She was a big girl. She could handle a fling in Venice. But was a fling without a future worth it?

Remaining as still as the night air that surrounded them, Carol stole a glance at Sergio from the corner of her eye. Sergio picked up on her stealth. He squeezed her hand and closed his eyes, offering a silent thanks to Paolo for calling in a favor and reserving this elegant gondola, with no time limit attached, on such short notice. Only a *Casanova* could have come up with such an idea. For all his years of being the man about town, dating the movers and shakers of Venice, showing up at all the right places, Sergio had never romanced anyone on this most romantic venue, a gondola ride to the Bridge of Sighs. He'd always played his cards conservatively, holding back his best hand. Tonight that would change. It had to. He was falling in love with Carol Duncan, *because* she was Carol Duncan.

"The Bridge of Sighs is a paradox," Sergio was saying, but Carol hardly heard him. She stared, open-mouthed, above her as the gondola stopped directly beneath the beautiful ornate expanse bathed in both natural moonlight and the many lamps gracing Rio del Palazzo, with its glassine water flowing gently below the famous bridge.

Sergio went on. "The condemned were marched from the Doge's Palace to the prison across this bridge, and they sighed, as the legend goes. They sighed because they knew it would be the last time they would see Venice. And yet, we believe that if lovers kiss beneath this Bridge of Sighs, their love will live on, happily ever after."

Carol was silent. Had she heard anything he was saying? Perhaps he could play Paolo's role tonight, a latter day Casanova, master of many seductive charms guaranteed to dissolve suspicions, fears, worries, and in their place create only the most perfect moments. Moments worthy of a kiss beneath this bridge.

"Are you ready for champagne?" the gondolier asked from the bow. "It is arranged." Another special touch thanks to Paolo that Sergio had not considered. But before he could answer the gondolier, Carol's lips had found his. Her kiss was warm and moist and soft. Sergio wrapped her in his arms. She closed her eyes, pressed herself against him, hungry for more.

Sergio was thrilled to oblige.

Chapter 16

Carol stretched her arms above her head, yawned, and opened her eyes to the morning sunlight that filtered through the sheer curtains hanging from the small window by the bed. Sergio's bed. She lowered her arms and turned on her side, watching him sleep. She kissed his pillow so as not to disturb him.

Without question, she'd had a fling last night. That's how she saw it up to now. She trembled, remembering her passion, the surprise in Sergio's eyes when she kissed him beneath the Bridge of Sighs. Her joy in abandoning all thought of protocol. And Sergio's response. Unbelievable. She hadn't been kissed like that since Evan. No, Sergio was better. Much better. His kisses *meant* something, she'd sensed this at once. And his lovemaking was—she closed her eyes as she searched for the perfect description—exquisite. Yes. That was what last night was. An exquisite fling. A fling of substance! She grunted. *Was there such a thing?*

She opened her eyes again to find Sergio propped on his forearm, his fingers gently combing through the ends of her hair, smoothing out the tangles.

"Did we embarrass that gondolier?" Carol whispered as she turned toward him from under the sheets. "We were making out like two kids at an unsupervised party!"

Sergio laughed. "Gondoliers see everything! Nothing phases them. Love is love. Besides"—he leaned back to reach for the unopened bottle of champagne from the night before—"I distinctly remember the last thing he did when he took us back here."

Carol wrinkled her brow. She barely remembered disembarking the gondola. "What did he do?"

Sergio winked twice. "This is what he did," he said. "One wink for you, and one wink for me. And he gave me the bottle of champagne, for later. Only, we got busy, you and I."

"We got busy," Carol repeated. *And I think we are about to get busy again*, her instincts told her. Sergio got off his forearm and placed his head on her pillow. He reached under the sheets to feel the warmth of her skin, the fullness of her breasts. Pulling her close, he kissed her long and hard. Again the bottle of champagne could wait.

***

Sergio had not given his staff any reason to anticipate a change in his routine. Still, no telephone call or text had come in from Cosimo or Fernando. *Perhaps they expected me to take some time off work*, Sergio reasoned, smiling at the ceiling. *Maybe you, Giacomo Casanova, tipped them off?* He kissed Carol softly so as not to wake her.

Carol had fallen asleep not caring if her family had sent any more texts or voicemails to her phone. How different the world looked now. How long had it been since she felt like this? And how wonderful it felt to give as much as to receive. Sergio's response to her touch, immediate and intense, met her need to respond in kind, to let him know that his happiness was hers.

In the span of mere days that seemed like a lifetime, she and Sergio crossed that fine line between having sex and making love. They'd reached the apex of their passion together, calling out to each other, holding fast to the moment, then melting together in a glorious spiral that transcended time and space.

They'd made love again this morning and fell again into a deep sleep, Sergio's moans of pleasure still pulsating through Carol, her urgent cries of joy filling Sergio's heart.

They remained locked in each other's arms late into the night, and Carol listened as Sergio told her a story that spanned a decade, about a young girl from long ago and what had happened to him because he could not let go of her. Not until now. When he finished, Carol lifted her head from his chest to face him. She felt him tense beneath her.

"I don't care whether you thought I looked like your old girlfriend or not," she said.

"You don't?" Sergio sat up and pulled her closer to him. "Anyone else would have thought I was *pazzo*! Crazy!"

"Well, I'm not anyone else, and you're not crazy," Carol replied. She hugged him hard. "I do have a question, though," she added.

Sergio felt reborn. He'd taken a chance and won. No question was too probing to threaten their connection now. "Ask me anything," he said, nestling his head on her pillow.

Carol closed her eyes. Her lips found Sergio's earlobe. She nibbled it playfully. "I hate to sound stupid," she whispered, "but what on Earth is a pied butcherbird?"

Chapter 17

"I want to introduce you to Giacomo Casanova," Sergio told Carol as they navigated the crowded expanse of Piazza San Marco. They were going to Bibi's, Sergio explained, where Paolo Trezzi was waiting, in full Casanova regalia.

He would solve Carol's dilemma, Sergio was sure of that. Paolo was a man of many talents, among those being a consummate fixer.

Sergio led Carol through the arch leading from Piazza San Marco to Paolo's neighborhood. Paolo met them outside Bibi's. He greeted Carol in true Casanova fashion, removing his cap, bowing deeply, kissing her hand.

"And now, Signorina, your wish is my command, as the genie says when he comes out of his lamp, yes?" Paolo circled around and between Carol and Sergio. "Tell me your wish, then. Casanova will see that you receive it!"

Carol turned to Sergio. "What's he talking about?" she asked him.

Sergio shrugged. "I guess he wants to help you,"

he offered.

"With what?" Carol pushed back. She felt herself becoming testy. Why did Italians always have to be so dramatic?

"With your decision," Paolo replied, still in Casanova mode. "You wish to stay in Venice, but you have to leave, yes?"

Carol nodded. "I have to go back to work. My vacation time is up."

"Like Cinderella at midnight, yes?" Casanova asked.

Carol frowned. "Sergio, let's go. This Casanova thing is like being under a light bulb in a police station." She turned to Paolo. "Thank you, Paolo, for trying to help, but there's no way I can stay in Venice. I have responsibilities in the States. My job is there, and my family. I can't just *not* go back."

Paolo dropped his act. He took off his cap and his cape. He and Sergio exchanged knowing glances.

"That is true! And Sergio wants to meet your family," Paolo said.

"Impossible," Carol replied. "My sister and her husband went home, and my brother and I leave tomorrow." Randy had sent a text just this morning:

Spending last day in Venice with V, meet u at airport XO ur bro.

Carol was happy to know Randy and Vicky had returned to Venice in time for Randy to make his flight, but she also knew his calendar was more flexible than hers was. Randy still had two more weeks off before his next construction job was to start. Carol was scheduled to be back in the ER the day after she returned home.

"I'm sorry, Paolo, there's no time." She took Sergio's hand. "We have today. Let's enjoy it." She forced a smile as her heart sank. Who knows when she would see Sergio again? If she were totally honest with the two men standing before her, she'd tell them how she really felt. She didn't want to share her time with Sergio with anyone, not even with her own family, on her last day in Venice. Paolo, however, seemed to read her mind.

"You two go on, I know you want time to yourselves." He winked at Carol, and assured Sergio that there would be nothing to worry about.

"I know some sympathetic people in the Customs and Immigration offices. They are great fans of Casanova. If I ask them to speed things up in the name of love, they will give your application top priority!"

Carol's eyes widened. "What application?"

"Mine. For a passport," Sergio replied. He felt his neck grow warm. He was some big man about town, all right. So sophisticated, so worldly, that he'd never traveled to another continent. His embarrassment spread to his face.

"Oh my. You've never had a passport," Carol murmured. "Not even to go look for your old girlfriend?"

"Never," Sergio answered gravely. "And I have no interest in going anywhere except where you go."

They strolled the Riva and bought gelato, then sat at the water's edge just as they had done that first day they met less than two weeks ago. It seemed like a lifetime had passed since then.

Sergio and Carol crossed arms and shared tastes of each other's cones. "I think I turned out to be the luckiest man in the world for staying right here in Venice," Sergio said. He noticed a smear of chocolate gelato just above her lips. "You have a little *baffi*, a little mustache," he joked. He kissed her then, melting the sweet residue with his lips. "I love you, you know, baffi and all."

Carol nestled in his arms as they watched the sun set over the Grand Canal.

"I *will* see you again, I promise," Sergio whispered as he drew Carol closer. She knew he would be true to his word, and to her.

"And I will be waiting for you. Only for you," Carol responded, meaning it with all her heart. "I still cannot believe this is not all a dream, that this is really happening."

Sergio couldn't believe it either. But it all felt so right. "Shall we blame it on Casanova, or on the Bridge of Sighs?" he asked, tightening his arm around her. Carol watched the gondolas glide past, one of them turning onto the Rio del Palazzo, over which the Bridge of Sighs held sentry, watching over all of the lovers who passed beneath its span. Could their love span an ocean?

Carol felt the magic of Venice wash over her as it had so many times before, only this time the magic was no illusion. She looked up at Sergio. He was waiting for her answer, his dark eyes filled with tears. Tears of such happiness she'd never known a grown man to show. Her heart felt close to bursting.

"Both," she said, just before his kiss left her speechless once more.

Epilogue: One Year Later

Carol was at the airport hours before Sergio's plane was scheduled to land. She'd had enough, pacing the floors in her apartment, waiting for the rain to stop. It was easier to just get in her car and drive extra slow to La Guardia. There was enough to do at the airport to pass the time besides watch the skies. She could check the Arrivals board between browsing the airport shops and grabbing lunch at the terminal food court. And, of course, she could read and re-read the wedding invitation.

Randy, of all people, getting married tomorrow! Carol still couldn't get over her baby bro taking the big plunge. He and Vicky would be honeymooning in Venice, where it all began for them just about this time last summer. Where had the time gone?

Carol was thrilled that Sergio was coming to the wedding. They'd planned a Christmas visit, but Sergio decided to fly in now. *You can't attend Randy's wedding unescorted. Besides, not seeing you for a whole year has been hell. All the technology in the world just don't do us justice.* Carol couldn't agree more. She was as tired as Sergio was of using ZOOM.

The announcement calling her to the Liberty Club desk interrupted her third cup of coffee. Carol wasn't a member of the exclusive frequent flyers' club. Elaine was, though. Could she be here? The last Carol heard, Elaine was getting her hair done this afternoon in preparation for tomorrow.

"I'm Carol Duncan." Carol handed the Liberty Club concierge her driver's license identification.

The concierge smiled broadly. "There is a message for you. Please. Come this way."

Carol followed the concierge. Why would anyone she knew leave a message for her at the Liberty Club? *Why not just text me?* she thought as the concierge led her into a small room with a few club chairs facing a large TV screen.

"Make yourself comfortable," the concierge said, still smiling as he closed the door softly, leaving Carol alone.

Carol stood in the middle of the room. *Make myself comfortable? There must be a mistake. I'm not even a member of this club. I don't get it.*

The TV screen suddenly turned a bright blue. Carol stepped back and slowly lowered herself into one of the chairs. *Probably a promotional message.* She lifted her phone from her purse. Elaine and Albert were Liberty Club members. *Maybe this was their idea.* Carol checked for a message from Elaine but found nothing in her text or voice messages. She put her phone away.

Carol looked up as the TV screen began to change, its blue background fading, replaced by an image of the Bridge of Sighs against a star-filled Venetian sky. Beneath its span, five words emerged shimmering upon the moonlit waters of the Rio del Palazzo:

Please Say Yes, Your Sergio.

END

Acknowledgements

My thanks to the editors at Blossom Spring Publishing, and to Ms. Claire Voet, Publishing Manager, for helping me see this book to fruition in the face of unforeseen circumstances that resulted in my having to ask for deadline extensions. The flexibility extended by BSP on my behalf is greatly appreciated.

To my readers, who have patiently waited for the next romantic location, I hope this little trip to Venice makes your day. Your enthusiasm always makes mine. *Mille grazie, tutti!*

About The Author

Harriet G. Fry was born in Philadelphia, Pennsylvania and is a Vietnam-Era veteran of the United States Navy. She holds a Master's Degree in Education and spent many years as a Special Education teacher with the School District of Philadelphia.

As a freelance writer, her articles and essays, ranging from how-to and hobbies, to travel, inspirational, and human interest, have appeared in a variety of magazines and newspapers in the United States. Harriet served on the Board of Directors of the Philadelphia Writers' Conference for over twenty years and was its president for a term in the early 2000s.

Widely traveled throughout the United States and abroad, Harriet enjoys attending live theatre, and swimming for exercise. She admits to one guilty pleasure: anything chocolate!

Harriet resides in Conshohocken, Pennsylvania.

For more information please visit
https://www.harrietgfryinprint.com/

Follow Author Harriet G. Fry on her official website,
and on LinkedIn
https://www.harrietgfryinprint.com/
https://www.linkedin.com/in/harriet-g-fry-16667358/

www.blossomspringpublishing.com